She shook her head. "My answer is no."

Of course it was, Dante thought, torn between exasperation and admiration. Most women, most *men*, in her position would be biting his hand off, but Talitha had a mile-wide streak of stubbornness equal only to his.

He shook his head. "As usual, you're turning something simple and straightforward into a drama."

She gave him an icy glare. "You want simple and straightforward, then how about goodbye? Or better still, ciao?"

"Ciao also means hello, *ciccia*," he said softly. "Another reason for joining me in Siena." He felt light-headed but also exhilarated, like a diver on the Fiordo di Furore looking down into the Tyrrhenian Sea. "Unless of course it was a slip of the tongue."

He watched her bite into her lower lip, suddenly aware of nothing beyond the beating of his heart and the darkening of her irises.

As the silence between them lengthened, he felt the tension mount.

Louise Fuller was a tomboy who hated pink and always wanted to be the prince—not the princess! Now she enjoys creating heroines who aren't pretty pushovers but are strong, believable women. Before writing for Harlequin, she studied literature and philosophy at university, then worked as a reporter on her local newspaper. She lives in Royal Tunbridge Wells with her impossibly handsome husband, Patrick, and their six children.

Books by Louise Fuller

Harlequin Presents

Craving His Forbidden Innocent
The Rules of His Baby Bargain
The Man She Should Have Married
Italian's Scandalous Marriage Plan
Beauty in the Billionaire's Bed

Christmas with a Billionaire

The Christmas She Married the Playboy

The Sicilian Marriage Pact

The Terms of the Sicilian's Marriage

Visit the Author Profile page
at Harlequin.com for more titles.

Louise Fuller

———

THE ITALIAN'S RUNAWAY CINDERELLA

HARLEQUIN® PRESENTS®

ISBN-13: 978-1-335-56843-4

The Italian's Runaway Cinderella

Copyright © 2022 by Louise Fuller

This edition published by arrangement with Harlequin Books S.A.

For questions and comments about the quality of this book, please contact us at CustomerService@Harlequin.com.

Harlequin Enterprises ULC
22 Adelaide St. West, 41st Floor
Toronto, Ontario M5H 4E3, Canada
www.Harlequin.com

Printed in U.S.A.

THE ITALIAN'S RUNAWAY
CINDERELLA

CHAPTER ONE

'RIGHT, SO I'LL speak to you later. Unless, of course, you want to go through it one more time?'

Shifting the phone against her ear, Talitha St Croix Hamilton bit down hard onto the pen between her teeth. It was the only way she could stop herself from screaming at her boss.

She had been flattered and surprised that Philip had asked her and not her more experienced colleague Arielle to meet with their prospective new client.

'I'm throwing you in the deep end,' he'd said by way of explanation. 'Might as well find out early on if you're going to sink or swim. Or just need armbands,' he'd added drily.

He had seemed unperturbed by his decision at the time, but now that the meeting was less than an hour away she wondered if he was starting to have second thoughts.

'Absolutely not,' she said firmly, with a flick of her long blonde ponytail. 'Really, truly, Philip. I've got this.'

'Good,' Philip said, equally firmly. 'My apologies

for the interrogation. I really do have complete faith in you, Talitha, but it's my name above the door so I need to be sure you're sure.'

A rush of gratitude moved through her veins. Philip Dubarry was a good boss. She liked him. He paid well. He treated his staff with respect. He was patient and generous with his time and knowledge. But he was also a control freak. A micromanager who found it hard to let go of the reins even briefly.

Although she couldn't really blame him.

For starters, she had only been working for him for seven months. Plus, she had a sneaking suspicion that she had only got the job in the first place because Philip had bought and sold paintings for her grandfather, Edward.

Back in the day, thanks to the success of her great-great-grandfather's engineering firm, her family had grown very rich, and their estate, Ashburnham, had quickly became home to one of the most important private art collections in England.

She took the pen out of her mouth and tossed it onto the desk.

Not anymore.

The St Croix Hamilton name still packed a punch socially, but most of the good art had been discreetly sold, and the once beautiful Georgian mansion was now falling into disrepair. Whatever money there had been was now owed in triplicate to the bank.

But she wasn't going to think about that now. She needed to bring her A game to this meeting with the

VIP. Her pulse danced nervously. Not easy when she didn't even know who she was meeting with.

She did know that they were intensely private and rich.

Very, very rich.

At least she was dressed for the part, in this season's Giles Deacon. Of course, it wasn't hers. The floor-length striped silk dress would have been heart-stoppingly expensive to buy outright, but she had found this place in Chelsea where they rented out designer dresses by the day for less than lunch at Kitty Fisher's.

And it was a good choice. Judging by the numerous admiring sideways looks she'd received as she'd walked down Bond Street in the warm, late June sunshine she wasn't the only one to think so. But for her it was more than just a stunningly beautiful dress. It was her armour.

Beneath she might be quaking, but nobody would ever know. Nor would they guess that the once mighty St Croix Hamiltons were defaulting on their loans or that the glistening diamonds hanging from her ears were actually exquisite fakes.

'You'll do fine.' Philip's voice snapped into her thoughts. 'Speak clearly. Smile as if you mean it. And most importantly of all remember that the client—'

'Is always right.' She finished the sentence for him, paused, then said as casually as she could manage, 'So we really know nothing about them?'

'Nothing at all. But that's why they come to us, Talitha. If they wanted a circus they would go to Broussard's.'

Philip sniffed dismissively down the phone and she smiled. Broussard's ran with all the big-name celebrity art collectors—the rock stars and actors and film directors who liked the hype of the auction.

But for those ultra-high net worth clients who preferred anonymity in their buying habits, there was only one dealer of choice in the world of high-end art acquisition. Philip was valued as much for his discretion as his expertise. And his reputation had paid enormous dividends. While smaller than most of the other dealers, he now had a stable of secretive but enormously wealthy collectors ranging from self-made tech magnates to royalty.

After Philip had hung up, Talitha flipped open her laptop and flicked through her presentation one more time. She so badly wanted this to go well. It wasn't exactly a promotion, but it would mean she could go back to the bank with something more than just her name for collateral.

It would prove that she had got this job through merit—that it wasn't just for show. And that she was taking their 'advice'. Working hard and being taken seriously at work. Surely that counted for something?

It *had* to count for something because she was running out of options.

Don't go there, she told herself. *Don't worry about what might never happen.*

Except it would happen. If she couldn't persuade the bank to extend the loan, then all of it would be gone for ever. The estate would be sold to the highest bidder and her grandfather would lose his home.

She pushed back against the lump building in her throat, steadied her breathing. He deserved more than that. He alone had done the right thing. He was the only person she had ever really trusted.

Her pulse skipped a beat. Or rather he was the only person deserving of her trust.

He had never let her down, and she wasn't going to let him down now. Whatever it took, she was going to get the bank to back off.

'Talitha?'

She glanced up. Philip's faultlessly professional PA, Harriet James, was hovering in the doorway. 'They're here. I'm just going to go down to Reception to greet them.'

'Thanks, Harriet. I'll see you in the studio.'

She was suddenly acutely conscious that she was trembling. More than trembling. Her whole body was quivering—like her grandfather's favourite spaniel Bluebell at a shoot.

But it was okay to be nervous, she told herself as she made her way upstairs. And she wasn't trembling just from nerves—she was excited too.

The studio was on the top floor, and it was her absolute favourite room in the building.

Thirty years ago, Philip had bought the first of the four adjoining townhouses that would eventually become his gallery and offices. The cavernous studio stretched across the length of all four of the houses, and as well as being a meeting room it doubled as a light-filled ever-changing showcase for Dubarry's collection of art, including her current favourite Cy Twombly 'Blackboard' painting.

Even on London's greyest days it was an uplifting, inspiring space. Hopefully, it would inspire her mystery buyer to reach deep into their cavernous pockets.

Her pulse twitched. She could hear footsteps and Harriet talking—very high and very fast, as if she was nervous. Talitha frowned. That was a first! Even when one of the workmen had accidentally set fire to the building during the recent redecoration of the offices the PA had maintained her Sphinx-like aura of calm.

Suddenly Talitha's body was quivering again. For Harriet to be that one edge it must be royalty. An emir, maybe, or perhaps the ruler of some European principality.

Smoothing her hair, she took a breath, pinned a smile to her face and turned as Harriet walked into the room followed by a group of dark-suited men.

But she only saw one.

For a few mindless seconds she stared at the tall, dark figure at the front, and then her smile froze to her face and she stood welded to the spot by a pain she had never felt before…a pain she couldn't even give a name to.

It wasn't him. It couldn't be, she told herself. Everybody had a twin in the world, and this must be his.

Harriet was still talking but her words were muffled and distorted, as if they were coming from underwater. Around her the lines of the room seemed to blur and sway. Only the man at the front stayed solid and clean-edged.

For the last few years hardly a day had gone by when she hadn't thought about him, or a night when he hadn't trespassed into her dreams.

But nothing could compare with the man himself. And, of course, now that he was here it made perfect sense that he should be her secretive collector.

Dante King.

Even at the embryonic stages of his career he had been reserved about his life. She had known he was close to his parents. He'd spoken briefly but often to both of them, always in Italian, and she had assumed his reticence to discuss them was down to his having a traditional Mediterranean protectiveness of his family. At the time his quiet but steady devotion had reminded her of her grandfather.

Of course, she had assumed that once they got to know one another better he would open up to her.

Her chest tightened.

What a joke. Despite supposedly planning for a future together, Dante had excluded her from his life, keeping her at arm's length from everyone who mattered to him.

Her stomach clenched. Knowing how much he cared about his family, she had glossed over her own useless parents, but she needn't have worried. He was only interested in people who could help him become master of the universe.

And now here he was, standing in the studio.

The richest man no one had ever heard of.

Every devastating inch of him.

From the mussed-up dark hair to the soles of his

handmade leather shoes. Staggeringly handsome, unequivocally male.

Once upon a time he had been the man she'd adored so much that it had hurt to be away from him even for a moment.

Her pulse trembled. He was also the man who had told her he loved her and then taken her heart and broken it into a thousand pieces.

A shiver ran through her body.

Three years ago, in a Milanese bar filled with boisterous, swaggering Italian men, he had turned heads with his quiet, serious beauty. And it wasn't just the flawless curves of his face. Back then there had been a hint of softness, a vulnerability beneath those sculpted cheekbones, that had made every woman in that bar—including her—glance over for a fraction longer than entirely necessary.

But she was a different person now.

Today she was under no illusions. She knew Dante King had no soft side, that he was a man on a mission. Single-minded, driven, relentless. Blinkered, by an empire-building ambition that had consumed his life, leaving no room for anything or anyone else. Including her.

Especially her.

Stomach lurching, she fixed her gaze on his coldly handsome face. And now he wasn't just a King in name. With his business empire straddling the globe, he ruled a metaphorical kingdom. Her breath caught in her throat. She had to admit, it suited him. He looked incredible. And utterly formidable.

Harriet cleared her throat. 'Mr King, I'd like to introduce you to our acquisitions associate, Talitha St Croix Hamilton.'

She gave a brisk nod in Talitha's direction.

'Talitha will be your guide, your counsel, your adviser. But here at Dubarry's we believe that the best advice we can give to collectors is to trust yourself and your taste. Your wishes are paramount. Whatever you want, we can get it for you.'

Dante lifted a smooth dark eyebrow. 'Anything I want?' he repeated.

Talitha swallowed hard as his grey eyes flickered in her direction. Now that the shock was fading she felt fragile, jumpy; her throat was dry and tight.

Harriet smiled. 'Even pieces that are not officially for sale. For example, last week Talitha had a client who wanted a black and white de Kooning. She found a collector in Japan who owned the painting. Then she found another, more important de Kooning in San Francisco. She sold that painting to the Japanese collector, and he sold his painting to our client.'

There was the tiniest of pauses, like a caught breath. A ghost of a smile played around his hard mouth. 'That's a rare talent,' he said coolly.

Talitha's chest squeezed tight. His face was impossible to read, but the achingly familiar sound of his voice, with the slight roll to his 'r's hinting at his Italian parentage, made her pulse accelerate so fast that she had to curl her toes inside her shoes to stop herself from turning and running for the door.

But then those piercing grey eyes intercepted her

light brown gaze and suddenly breathing, much less running, was impossible as, inclining his head fractionally, he subjected her to an agonisingly slow, searching appraisal that sped up her already racing pulse.

'Ms Hamilton. How have you been?'

There was a beat of silence.

'You two know each other?' Harriet's curious gaze jumped back and forth between them like a metronome.

Known. Loved. Lost, she thought, fighting the wild beating of her heart as a curl of anger and misery tugged at the rapidly fraying threads of her self-control.

For perhaps a fraction of a second she thought she saw a flicker of something in his cool grey eyes…a primitive darkening that made it difficult to breathe. Then it was gone, and she was left wondering if, like everything else about their relationship, it had been a figment of her imagination.

'No, I wouldn't say that,' he said slowly. 'But our paths did cross briefly. Back in the day.'

She forced herself to meet the challenge in his eyes.

That was one way of putting it. Another might be that he had played her. He had seen the weakness in her, but not bothered exploring the reason behind it. Instead, like all successful predators, he had exploited it with the ruthless efficiency that had made him one of the youngest billionaires in history.

His business, KCX, was not the largest yet, but it was the fastest growing digital asset exchange in the world, and its stratospheric rise should have made its creator and CEO a household name. But Dante King avoided publicity and rarely gave interviews.

That didn't mean you should underestimate him, though, she thought, her senses primed for fight or flight as his eyes locked with hers. Not if her experience was anything to go by.

Had he ever cared for her? Or had it all been about her connections?

Her pulse trembled as he turned his head minutely in Harriet's direction.

'Ms James… Gentlemen… Could you give us the room, please? I'd like to talk to Ms Hamilton in private.'

He spoke quietly, and there was nothing in his face to give even the slightest clue to his thoughts, but there was unmistakable authority to every word and within seconds they were alone.

Suddenly the huge room seemed airless, small.

Talitha felt every muscle tense. Given how many times she'd played out this scene in her head, she should have used up all her anger and frustration. But as the door clicked softly shut she felt a wave of rage rise up inside her and, spinning towards him, she went straight on the attack.

'What are you doing here? It's been three years, Dante.'

Her throat tightened. Three years of hiding from the past. Hiding from her feelings. Three years of trying to put her shattered life back together. People said that time was a great healer, but their hearts hadn't been trampled on by Dante King.

He took a step forward, the overhead lights carving a shadow beneath his cheekbones. 'I know how long it's been, Talitha.'

Watching his mouth form the syllables of her name made her skin grow hot and tight. 'Well, you've wasted your time.' Her heart was hurling itself against her ribs so hard that she thought it might burst through her chest.

He had left her behind when he'd gone to visit his family and like a fool she had sat and waited for him.

And waited. And waited.

Three whole weeks without a word.

Given how her parents had acted, you would have thought she'd know better, but she had been in thrall to her fantasy of love. So in thrall she would probably still be sitting there waiting if she hadn't bumped into Nick and found out the truth. That Dante had used her for who she knew—not wanted her for who she was.

Afterwards, she had spent months trying to live without him. Months hating him.

Did he really think that he could just turn up out of the blue after all this time and ask to talk to her in private? Who *did* that?

Glancing over at his unforgivably handsome face, she felt acid burn in her throat. Someone without a compassionate bone in his body, that was who.

She shook her head. 'We're not going there. Not now, not ever. If you wanted to talk then maybe you should have thought about it at the time. But you didn't.'

Didn't. Wouldn't. *Couldn't.*

She banked down her misery, remembering the tautness of his jaw. He literally couldn't say the words. And it wasn't as if he'd tried to fix things afterwards. She had thought he might, hoped he would. But he had not so much as texted her.

He stared at her in silence, considering her words, considering his response, and she felt her stomach lurch again. She knew his tricks, knew how he used silence as a weapon, watching, waiting for her to lose the thread of her argument.

Well, this time he could wait—just as she had waited in his apartment.

'There was nothing to talk about. You overreacted—as usual.'

Her fingers curled instinctively into fists. *Overreacted—as usual.* She gaped at him, stunned at his careless tone. She had been trying to save their relationship.

'I'd rather overreact than underwhelm,' she snapped.

Something flashed in his dark eyes, and when he spoke his voice was dangerously soft. 'I'm sorry to disappoint you again, but I didn't come here to talk to you, Talitha.' He moved past her, stopping in front of a striking geometric Frank Stella canvas. 'In fact, I wasn't aware that you were employed by Dubarry's.'

It took a moment for his words to sink in.

So it was just a coincidence?

Her breathing jerked and she felt her face grow warm. What had she been thinking? Three years ago Dante had proved unequivocally that he didn't care about her. She had known then that he was a heartless, self-serving bastard, so why had she thought he'd come looking for her?

She clenched her teeth. Because misjudging him was an art she'd perfected.

'You were never aware of me.'

He didn't turn around and she stared at his back, her heart hammering against her chest. He had been standing like that in the bar in Milan the first time they'd met, and she should have seen it as an omen—a sign of things to come: Dante looking the other way, his attention fixed on the horizon, on a future that didn't include her.

She should have had more sense than to get involved with him in the first place, but she had let her body override her brain, let her libido quash common sense and the evidence of her parents' miserable marriage and allowed her gaze to hover on the loose curl of dark hair grazing the collar of his T-shirt and on the definition of muscle beneath the thin fabric.

Silky soft and hard.

The contradiction had fascinated her, excited her, then and even more so afterwards, when they had gone to bed and she had slid her hands through his hair and he had rolled her under his hard body, his mouth urgently seeking hers—

She blinked the image away determinedly, unwilling to dwell on his memorable skills in that area.

'I was always just background noise.'

He turned then, his dark gaze resting on her face, his brooding, masculine presence somehow filling the massive studio.

'You were never in the background. You lit up the room.'

He took a step closer—too close. Now she could see the contours of his muscles beneath the deep blue shirt and superbly fitted suit jacket.

'Like sunlight. Only you shone all day and night. Sometimes I used to think that maybe you were a star that had fallen to earth.'

His words made her pulse flutter. 'Don't do that.' She glared at him, her cheeks flushed with colour. 'Don't pretend that our relationship was about anything but sex.'

Her voice dried up for a second as her brain unhelpfully reminded her of the sex they had shared. She didn't have words for what it had been like with him. But she didn't need words. Just remembering the scratch of his stubble against her throat as he'd thrust inside her sent ripples of pleasure through her body.

Blanking her brain, she forced her eyes up to his. 'And even that was probably a sidebar. What you really liked was my name.'

'Not true.' He took a step closer. 'I didn't know your name when I saw you in that bar. I didn't know anything about you except that you were the most beautiful woman I'd ever seen.' Reaching out, he caught a stray strand of hair between his fingers. 'You know, if Hera and Athena and Aphrodite had been sitting beside you, I would still have given you the golden apple.'

His touch made her tremble inside. She felt a flicker of heat low down in her belly, as if her body was coming to life, waking from a long hibernation. And suddenly she was tantalisingly aware of his hand with its smattering of tiny hairs, and of the enticingly masculine smell that she associated only with Dante.

There was a temptation to move closer, to lean into his hand and rub against it like a cat, and she hated herself for still feeling that need. She badly wanted to take a step back, put some distance between them, only she was damned if she was going to so much as hint that a part of her still craved him.

Ignoring the traitorous quivering of her body, she forced herself to hold her ground. 'I don't like apples,' she lied. 'I prefer pears. But I wouldn't expect you to know that because you weren't interested in me. I was just a stepping stone.'

'I thought you didn't want to talk about the past.' His grey eyes rested steadily on her. 'Careful, Talitha, you're breaking your own rules.'

She felt a tingly shiver scamper across her skin as his gaze dropped to the tiny pulse jerking in her throat.

'But then I seem to remember you making a habit of that.'

Cheeks flaming, she flinched inside—a fast, uncontrollable twitch. She knew what he was talking about. Those first few weeks in Milan had been wild, crazy. They hadn't been able to keep their hands off each other. It had been like an addiction, both of them never satisfied, always wanting more.

She breathed in sharply, blinking away a memory of the two of them on the staircase leading up to her hotel room, the fever-heat of his skin, her teeth nipping his shoulder in frustration as she squirmed against the hard swell of his erection pushing against his trousers.

Her fingers twitched into fists. Moments earlier she had wanted a fight. She had wanted to fight him, to hurt him as he had hurt her, but now she just wanted him to go. She needed him to go before she did something stupid. Like hit him.

Or kiss him.

Her chin tilted a little. 'I think you and I have very different memories of our time together, Dante. But, as you've already pointed out, you didn't come here to talk to me. You're here to discuss a strategy for your art collection.'

His gaze didn't shift from hers. 'That's correct.'

'Okay, then.'

She smiled at him coolly and would have marched out with her head held high if Dante hadn't made a slight sideways move to block her.

Her eyebrows shot up. 'What do you think you're doing?'

'I could ask you the same thing,' he said softly.

'I would have thought it was obvious.' Her chest rose and fell in time to the rapid beating of her heart. 'This meeting is over. If you wouldn't mind waiting, I'll go and find my colleague, Arielle Heathcote. She's very experienced—'

'But I do mind.'

Her skin was prickling, and she suddenly felt hot. It was bad enough that he had used her to further his ambitions. She didn't want to be demoted into a minion helping him in the pursuit of his latest hobby.

'What do you mean?' she demanded.

'I mean that you don't need to find your colleague. In this instance, you will suffice.'

She stared at him mutely, her heart hammering against her ribs, his barbed words scratching across her skin.

'You're just saying that to make things difficult. Clearly we can't work together.'

'We can't?' He frowned. 'What's your objection?'

His question sucked the breath from her lungs. He was still maddeningly calm and detached, and she knew that he was toying with her, pressing against the bruise. And suddenly she hated him—and hated herself for feeling another bubbling rush of irritation and anger.

For feeling anything.

'Objections, plural. I have many.'

The change in him was so subtle that if she had been a stranger she might have missed the slight narrowing of his dark eyes as he stared at her in silence.

'Perhaps you'd care to share them with me?'

His voice was still soft but Talitha felt the hairs stand up on the back of her neck. She deliberately hadn't followed his skyrocketing career, but occasionally, usually when she'd spent one too many evenings in, watching box sets and feeling like a modern-day Miss Havisham, she'd looked him up on the internet, and she knew he had a reputation for being someone you wanted as a friend, not an enemy.

But it was too late to worry about that.

'I don't care to share anything with you, Dante,'

she said hoarsely, the flickering resentment and misery that had been smouldering ever since he'd walked into the room catching fire. When had he ever shared anything with her? 'You know perfectly well why we can't work together. We have a history, a past.'

He shrugged. 'Exactly. It's in the past. If I'm willing to put it behind me, I fail to see why you shouldn't.'

She gaped at him, rendered speechless by his casual dismissal of her pain.

Put it behind her?

Her hand went instinctively to her throat, as if to protect herself from the impact of his words. Had their relationship really affected him so little?

Surely he must have known how much she'd loved him. Had he no idea how badly he had hurt her? Didn't he care even a little bit? Feel anything?

Her gaze fixed on his superbly tailored suit, the crisp blue shirt and discreetly patterned silk tie. In a word: no.

Dante King didn't do feelings. Particularly not other people's.

Suddenly she wanted to hurl herself at him, pummel him with her fists—anything to make him feel a fraction of her pain.

'We were engaged, Dante. You made a promise to me.'

A forever promise…a perfect moment in time.

Only that was all it had been: a moment.

His gaze slammed into hers and she tensed, her heart lurching as he stepped towards her.

'As did you.'

He was right. Only for her it had been more than a promise. It had been a leap of faith. As it turned out, it had been a leap too far.

'Everyone makes mistakes, Dante.' And she was still paying. Every day. 'Thinking that you and I could ever work was mine. And maybe this time it's business, not personal, but I'm not willing to make the same mistake twice.'

CHAPTER TWO

DANTE STARED AT Talitha in silence. She was wrong. This *was* personal.

Walking into the room, seeing her again after all these years, he had felt as though he had stepped through the looking glass into a world where nothing made sense. For one delirious moment he had actually thought he was asleep, and that all of it—this studio, the paintings, Talitha—was part of some elaborate dream.

It was the shock of seeing her again, he reassured himself grimly. Obviously he hadn't expected to see her.

His pulse twitched.

Maybe if he hadn't spent the last three years doing everything in his power to erase her from his memory then seeing her again might not have hit him so hard. But the shock of her beauty had felt like a bomb blast. Skin as smooth and pale as the inside of a shell…eyes the colour of fresh honeycomb…light blonde hair… and a perfect pink mouth like a rose opening to the morning sun.

Three years ago that was how he'd thought of her: his English rose.

His chest tightened.

Except she wasn't his anymore.

Now she belonged to another man.

He felt a tremor run through his body. That she had broken off their engagement had been agonising enough, but to find out that she had so quickly and casually replaced him still brought an acid rush of misery and resentment.

Had he been just a sticking plaster for her ego? A stopgap to pass the time? Or had it been a set-up from the start? A carefully choreographed illusion designed to get her ex jealous enough to propose? Either way, he had been a humiliatingly willing patsy and Talitha had got her man.

Although she had chosen to keep the St Croix Hamilton name professionally…

But that was Talitha all over, he thought, his anger and frustration spiralling up inside him in a vortex of emotion. She might look like a princess, but despite her aristocratic ancestors first and foremost she was a hard-boiled pragmatist, and while her husband was almost certainly rich, her surname had the country house cachet that opened the right kind of doors.

Three years ago he hadn't really understood that about her. He had been blinded by her beauty, astonished that a woman like her had even noticed him, let alone wanted to marry him. He'd been dazzled by everything about her so that he hadn't really been able to see her properly, much less analyse her behaviour or make judgements about her.

And she had seemed such a good person—wanting the best for him, for everyone.

His stomach clenched, as it always did when he thought back to the moment when he'd realised she had left him. Of course, he had tried calling her, but her phone had been switched off, and as shock and hurt had faded, anger had set in. By the time he had calmed down enough to accept that he couldn't live without her, weeks had passed and she was already engaged.

Hurt and humiliated, he had put the whole disastrous episode out of his head. It was only later that it had started to make sense. When he'd realised that she had wanted the best, and in Milan he had been the best on offer.

Until he'd left. And then she'd gone and found a better 'best'.

And now here she was, doing it for a living.

He gritted his teeth.

In business—in life—he liked to be prepared, and as usual his people had thoroughly researched Dubarry's. But for once he had failed to read their report in full.

It was a rare moment of sloppiness. Inexplicable and unacceptable. And in those first few devastating moments, when he'd seen Talitha and realised the consequences of that sloppiness, he'd been on the cusp of cancelling the whole meeting. But then he'd seen the flush of temper colouring her cheekbones, and the fire in her eyes, and just like that all thoughts of leaving were forgotten.

A knot formed in his stomach. She had no right to be angry. She wasn't the one who had been played like a puppet, then discarded.

But he wasn't the same love-struck fool he'd been three years ago. Then, he'd been in thrall to her. Now he was the one calling the shots, and this meeting would be over when he said it was.

'It's not really your decision, though, is it?' he said softly, his eyes locking with hers, holding her captive. 'As your colleague said, my wishes are paramount. In other words, what I want, I get. And I want you to curate my collection.'

She glared at him. 'You're doing this on purpose, aren't you?'

As her chin jutted forward he had a sudden intense urge to lean forward and cover her mouth with his. 'I'm not doing anything,' he said blandly.

'Yes, you are.' Her eyes flashed with temper and frustration. 'You're doing this because you didn't know I was going to be here, and you don't like being put on the spot, so you've decided to punish me.'

Her choice of words made his chest grow tight, his groin hot and hard. 'If I was going to punish you, *ciccia*, you wouldn't be standing here fully clothed. In fact, you wouldn't be standing at all.'

There was a long, twitching silence.

Gazing over at her pale face, he could see her mind racing, her thoughts tumbling over themselves as she struggled to think of a suitable reply. Finally, she looked up at him, her brown eyes wary and defensive, like a vixen cornered by a stray hound.

'Look, we need to deal with this like grown-ups,' she said stiffly. 'We both know that I can't work for you. Just think about what it would mean. Building a collection takes time. It's an ongoing process. And for me to best meet your needs it would require a connection, an intimacy—'

Her voice faltered and he knew that, like him, she was remembering the intimacy they had shared. His pulse accelerated. Back then, intimacy had meant more than being close; being with her had obliterated the boundaries of skin and bone. They had been like one person, their bodies dissolving, merging with desire. In her arms, even the past had been erased.

Only then she had left him, and she had erased their future too.

'In other words, nothing we haven't done before,' he said coolly.

He heard her take a breath.

'And look how that worked out,' she said.

'It worked just fine until you broke off our engagement.'

His words ricocheted around the silent room like gunfire.

'How can you say that?' She was looking at him in disbelief, as if he had suddenly sprouted scales. 'How can you say that to my face?'

'Quite easily. You were the one to leave.' His shoulders stiffened. The memory of returning to their empty apartment was hauntingly vivid still.

'That's not what happened.'

Banking down his anger, he fixed his gaze on her

beautiful deceitful face. 'And what about you, getting engaged to someone else just months after breaking off our engagement? I suppose that didn't happen either,' he said silkily.

She flinched, as if his words had struck her like a physical blow. Her eyes were wide and stunned. 'What are you…? How do you know about that?'

He shrugged. 'People talk.'

Actually, it had been one person in particular talking. The man she had been dating before they met. The man she had gone on to marry. But it had been humiliating enough at the time, finding out Talitha was engaged to someone else. He certainly wasn't about to replay the grim details of that conversation with her now.

'Well, I don't want to talk about it.'

He could feel his face hardening—could feel anger and pain seeping through his body, turning it to stone. After all this time it was still all about *her*, what *she* wanted.

'You left me,' he continued remorselessly. 'You went back to England and you got engaged to the man you were seeing before me. Which was the plan all along, I suppose.'

'I don't know what you're talking about.' She was shaking her head. 'There was no plan.'

He stared at her, anger hammering against his skin like hailstones. What was it about this woman that turned him inside out? It was all he could do not to reach over and shake her, and he tried to remember that he was a business titan who had earned a reputation for never letting emotion govern his actions.

'So what was the problem?' he said curtly. 'Was he dragging his feet? Did he need a little nudge in the right direction? Some off-stage rival for your hand?'

Her eyes flashed with anger, the irises darkening. 'It wasn't like that,' she shot back.

'Tell me, then. What *was* it like?'

What was he like? Did he make your body arch beneath him as you called his name? Did you tear each other's clothes from your bodies like animals?

His pulse was beating out of time, and he wanted to grab her by her arms and demand that she answer, but the words remained locked in his throat.

'It was nothing. It was just a rumour that got out of hand.'

He studied her face. There was more to it than she was letting on, but he couldn't deny the relief which washed over him as she shook her head.

'So you didn't marry him?' He couldn't bring himself to say the name.

'No, I did not. Although that actually comes under the heading of "None of your Business".'

Eyes blazing with fury, she took a step forward, jabbing a finger into his chest. 'In fact, nothing I do is any of your business anymore.'

He reacted instinctively, capturing her wrists, and she took a quick breath like a gasp as the movement tipped her forward against his body.

His pulse jumped, his heart running wild as he stared down into her mute, trembling, upturned face.

He could feel the heat of her skin through the thin silk of her dress and suddenly his whole existence was fixed on the ache in his groin. Or rather the need to satisfy it by pulling Talitha closer and kissing her until that quivering fury turned to a different kind of heat.

And then what?

Blanking his mind to the incessant clamouring of his body, he loosened his hands and took a step backwards. He'd lost control one too many times with this woman. It wasn't going to happen again.

Recalibrating his own sense of balance, he straightened his cuffs, then glanced past her, his eyes moving unhurriedly across the artworks, returning to settle on his favourite—a Twombly 'Blackboard' with its distinctive looping lines.

'Let me give you some advice, Talitha. You have a good job with a good company. If you want to keep it, I suggest you learn to separate your private life from your professional one.'

'You can talk,' she retorted. She had clearly recovered her poise and her voice. 'You never stopped working the entire time we were together.'

Heart thumping, he stared at her in mute frustration. 'Because, unlike you, I *had* to work.'

And not just to earn a living. He had needed to build an entire life from the bottom up—an unbreachable citadel that would shield him from the shame and ugliness of his past. Not that he'd expected Talitha, with her trust fund and her friends in high places, to understand that. She had never lived like normal people did: cooking, cleaning, working…

He looked over to where she was standing, fists clenched, eyes watching him warily.

Until now.

'And yet here you are,' he said slowly. 'A wage-slave.' Although she could just as easily be hosting brunch on the deck of some glossy boat, he thought, his gaze drifting appraisingly over her sweeping yacht-perfect silk dress. 'So, did you get bored of shopping and partying?'

He gazed around the huge studio space. 'Or is this your Hameau de la Reine? Do you come here to play at being a shepherdess?'

Watching her clench her teeth, he was surprised to find that he was enjoying himself. More than enjoying himself. He had been dazed when he'd seen her standing there, but now he felt clear-headed, invigorated, filled with a kind of fierce energy that made him feel almost superhuman.

His heart thudded. Talitha had been right. He had wanted to punish her, to taunt her with his power. Only what had started as just a whim had turned into something more insistent, more purposeful.

The truth was, he'd thought he was over her. But being in her orbit again was making it abundantly clear that she had simply stayed dormant in his blood—like a virus. Why else had seeing her again produced in him such an intense, uncontrollable sexual reaction?

But that was unacceptable. His past was an over-crowded place as it was. Being born into the notorious Cannavaro clan was a legacy he was still trying to outrun. It was why he worked so hard, why he kept his private life out of the spotlight.

It was also why he'd left Talitha behind in Milan.

Letting her meet his parents would have been too risky. All it would have taken was for her to find out he was adopted and then it would have been question after question, each one leading inevitably back to his ignominious birth.

And after what had happened when that man had snatched her bag, he had been even more desperate to get away from her. Losing control like that had not just scared him—it had made him question himself. Question who he was and whether he could tie Talitha ''till death do us part' to that man.

The irony was that when he'd been over in the States he had finally made up his mind to tell her everything—only to return and find her gone.

Even now the thought of how close he'd come to revealing the truth to her made his skin sting with humiliation. He didn't need any more bad memories. What he needed was to confront the past head-on by putting Talitha in her place, and in so doing free himself from any remaining hold she had over him.

'I'm not playing at anything. This is my job.'

Her voice was shaking, and the delicate hollows of her nostrils flared in time with her breathing. He knew that she was fighting to get on top of her temper.

'A job you got on merit alone, I suppose?' he said softly. 'Or did some friend of the family put in a good word?'

She was quivering with fury. 'It doesn't matter how I got this job. It's why I've still got it that counts.'

He let his gaze drift tauntingly across her beautiful angry face, down over the mouth-watering contours of her silhouette. 'And why is that, do you think?'

'It's because I'm good at it. Very good at it, in fact. Not that I'd expect you to believe that.'

He didn't. It was obvious Talitha had batted her eyelashes at Philip Dubarry to acquire her job.

'Why wouldn't I believe it?' His eyes locked with hers. 'As I recall, you did a lot of things extremely well.'

A flurry of pink rose over her collarbone and he felt a tiptoeing rush of excitement as he remembered just how well. Their relationship had been a long, scorching burn of a passion so obliterating and intense that for a short while it had consumed them both.

Was it any surprise that the embers were still warm?

For years he'd told himself that he was done with her, but now he knew he would never be over her unless he faced her on his own terms. He had no intention of rekindling that fire, of course. But knowing that he could make Talitha jump through a few hoops was immensely satisfying.

Enjoying the feeling of being in control, he held out his hand. 'I think we're done here.'

Ignoring his hand, she raised her head. 'We were done three years ago.'

Wrong, he thought silently, unable to drag his gaze away from the soft, kissable mouth that was currently pressed into a thin line of hostility. *They were just getting started.*

He stared at her, letting the silence between them lengthen, letting the tension mount. 'My people will be in touch,' he said finally.

Her eyes found his. 'I'll tell Arielle to expect their call.'

He heard the catch in her voice, the nervous edge, the flicker of relief, and he paused for a few seconds, as if weighing up possibilities. But really, he just wanted to string out the moment for just a little longer. Give her a chance to enjoy the feeling...

And then take it away.

'That won't be necessary,' he said slowly. 'Like I said earlier, I have no problem working with you. In fact...' he gave her a small taunting smile '...I'm looking forward to it. So, shall we say Friday? One-thirty? I'm staying at the Hanover. We can discuss my wishes in more detail over lunch.'

Her chin jerked upwards and he watched the conflicting emotions flit across her face, anger giving way to confusion and then panic. She was shaking her head now.

'That's not going to happen, Dante, so why don't you stop with all the games?'

He took a step forward, his eyes slamming into hers. 'I'm not playing games, Talitha. Not playing at anything. And neither will you be. You're going to be working. Hard. For me. Unless, of course, you want to explain your reasons for not doing so to your boss. Although I think that might end badly for you.'

Recently he had experienced a dust storm while on business in Saudi Arabia, and the hush that followed this remark reminded him of the long, grainy silence that had followed that storm.

'Nothing to say?' he murmured, knowing he had the upper hand. 'No last-minute tantrum or threat of bodily harm? Then I'll send a car to pick you up.'

And, indifferent to the shocked expression on her face, he turned and sauntered casually out of the room with the same unruffled authority with which he'd entered it.

Shifting against the cool leather, Talitha gazed out of the window, feeling her heart accelerate as the car nosed its way through the lunchtime traffic. She had been rather hoping that this was one commitment Dante wouldn't honour, but when she'd walked out of Dubarry's offices into the bright June sunshine the dark limousine had been hovering by the kerb like a dozing panther.

It was entirely unnecessary.

Given the traffic, it would probably take much the same time, or perhaps even less, to walk the point nine of a mile to the Hanover. But then Dante's motive for sending the car was not about logistics. It was just another little reminder that he was calling the shots.

As the limo took a left into Berkeley Square she stared enviously at the tourists sprawled lazily on the grass in the familiar oval gardens. Despite being in the heart of London, beneath the canopy of plane trees the garden was a green zone of quiet and calm.

Which was more than could be said for the inside of her head.

Her heartbeat faltered. This week was officially turning into the week from hell. And, given her past, that was saying something.

She silently ticked off the other contenders. There had been the week when she was seven and her father had decided to run off with the mother of her best friend from school. Then fast-forward six months to another week, another bombshell. This time her mother had collected her from school and announced that she was moving to Switzerland before dumping her with her grandparents. A year later her grandmother had died, and since then it had been just her and her grandfather.

Her throat clogged with tears, as it always did these days when she thought about Edward. He was not an overly affectionate man, but he had taught her to ride and shoot, and later how to make a perfect martini and to drive, quietly issuing instructions as she'd rumbled nervously around the estate in the gamekeeper's ancient Land Rover. He had taken her to the opera, and Royal Ascot, and most important of all he had shared with her his passion for art.

She felt her breathing hitch. Everything that was good about her life—about her—was thanks to him, and now she was going to take everything he loved, everything he needed, away from him.

Catching sight of her reflection, she felt her pulse stumble as she replayed her meeting at the bank. A casual observer would only see what she wanted them to see: the delicate features, the careless tilt to her chin.

But of course Charles Tait was not just a casual observer. He was an old family friend.

He was also a banker—in fact, he *was* the bank. And it was as the CEO of Taits that he had sat opposite her in his office and told her that he could see no reason other than sentiment to justify extending her grandfather's loan. And unfortunately he couldn't expect that sentiment to be shared by the other directors.

Remembering the apologetic smile that had accompanied his words, Talitha breathed out shakily. Maybe if she hadn't still been reeling from her encounter with Dante the day before she might have rallied, might have fought harder, but as soon as she'd sat down she'd had to press her hands into the arms of her chair to stop the feeling that the ground was tilting beneath her.

She had options. She could sell the townhouse.

Only that wouldn't be enough to save Ashburnham. It would be more sensible to sell the estate and keep the townhouse. Or better still sell both. That had been Charles's advice, and deep down she knew that he was right, but…

Blinking back tears, she tried to keep her breathing steady. She didn't want to cry. Not here. Not now. Not when she was only minutes away from meeting Dante.

Her heart thudded against her ribs and then, before she could change the direction of her thoughts, she was back to reliving the moment she had been trying so hard to not think about.

When Dante had strolled into the studio four days ago she hadn't known whether to scream or cry. It had taken her three years—three, long, miserable years—

but she had finally managed to forget what they had shared. Her infatuation, their engagement, his rejection.

Or she thought she had forgotten it.

But by the time he'd strolled out sixty minutes later it had been as though those years had never happened. Everything had suddenly been cut loose, every memory, every feeling…

Stomach tensing, she replayed those few tense seconds when she'd jabbed her finger into the hard wall of his chest and he had caught her hands and tugged her forward. He had been so close—close enough that she had been able to see the streaks of anger on his high, flat cheekbones, close enough to feel the heat of his skin.

For what had felt like an endless moment she had been rooted to the floor, legs trembling, hands shaky and incompetent. Only it had been more than just his tantalising proximity that had made time come to a quivering halt and her body lose substance. There had been a kind of restrained power and measured control in his grip, so that even as she'd fought to keep her footing, she'd been aware that he was *permitting* her to do so.

The promise to go further, to tip her against him and kiss her to the point of meltdown, made her breath catch in her throat. Had he done so she would have slapped his face and told him exactly where he could put his art collection.

Or would she?

It was a question she had been asking herself ever

since he had strolled out of the studio and, truthfully, she still wasn't sure that the answer would be yes.

Her heartbeat faltered a little as the limousine slowed and she caught a glimpse of the Hanover's iconic Art Deco façade.

All week she had been telling herself that she wasn't going to go through with it. Each morning she woke early, planning ways to tell Philip the truth, or as much of the truth as she could bear, and every night she left work having said nothing and feeling diminished by her own cowardice.

Her jaw clenched. She hated being the kind of person who let fear guide her behaviour. Dante might have been just pushing her buttons when he'd said that she needed to keep her personal life separate from work, but she knew he was right. She also suspected that Philip would agree with him.

And, really, was it such a big deal? It would be an hour or two at the most in a crowded restaurant, she thought as the car slowed. After that, in all probability she would never have to see him in person again. According to Philip, Dante conducted most of his business from his offices in New York. Besides, she knew him—and, whatever he might have said to the contrary, he didn't want her to work for him. He had summoned her here today solely because he wanted to rub in the fact that he could. Once he'd had his fun, he'd leave her alone.

So all she needed to do was get through this lunch and then it would be over.

Taking a breath, she smoothed down the skirt of her yellow silk dress, feeling calmer than she had in days.

'Good afternoon, Ms Hamilton.'

As she slid out of the car, a young man in a dark suit stepped forward.

'My name is Thomas. I work for Mr King in London. If you'd like to come this way?'

Smiling stiffly, she followed him inside.

The Hanover was her favourite London hotel.

As a child, she had often gone there for afternoon tea with her grandfather, but she hadn't been for a while, and she was slightly concerned that a recent makeover might have muddied the hotel's character. But, gazing anxiously across the legendary Art Deco foyer, she saw that the renovations were both sensitive and stylish, opulent but not overwrought. Everything looked sharp and clean and bright.

Her relief was swiftly replaced by a spasm of unease as the sleek brunette behind the reception desk glanced over at her curiously.

She felt her throat tighten.

What was she thinking?

Was she looking over because guests for the King suite were a rarity? Or had she sat there day after day watching a steady stream of women pass by on their way to Dante's rooms?

Not that she cared, she thought with a swift stab of anger. *They were welcome to him.*

As befitted a King, Dante was staying in the Royal Suite, and as she stepped out of the lift into the private lobby she lifted her chin like a gladiator on the threshold of the arena.

This was just a job, she told herself firmly as Thomas opened the door, then melted into the shadows. Dante was just a client. Thanks to her grandfather, and to Philip, she had a home, a career, a life. And even if that life overlapped briefly with his again, there was no way she was going to let Dante mess it up a second time.

The suite was every bit as opulent as its name suggested. *Rouge noir* velvet and sumptuous silks blended regal grandeur with contemporary comfort. But she barely registered her magnificent surroundings. Instead her entire attention was fixed on the man standing by the window.

He had his back to her. Deliberately? But of course, she thought, her mouth thinning in irritation. This whole charade was a deliberate show of power.

She gritted her teeth. In the past, like most people in love, she hadn't noticed his flaws. Or rather she had made them into positives, even telling herself in those moments when she'd felt him withdraw from her that they were proof of his sensitivity rather than evidence of his indifference.

But she wasn't that same dazzled, love-struck young woman anymore, and whatever power Dante had over her was temporary—*hopefully*. It existed only within the realms of a work-based relationship. She had moved on emotionally and physically.

He turned towards her and, looking at his mouth, she felt her pulse stutter. A betraying colour flooded her cheeks as she remembered again that moment in the studio and her body's traitorous response to his.

It was just a tic, she reassured herself quickly. An urge triggered by some muscle memory from the time when they hadn't been able to keep their hands off one another. But it wouldn't happen again.

'Talitha.'

He didn't smile, or make any attempt to shake her hand, instead he just stood there, gazing intently at her in a way that made her feel suddenly and acutely conscious of the beating of her heart and where the silk of her dress clung to her body.

'Dante,' she replied with a curt flick of her head. 'Wouldn't it have been easier just to meet in the restaurant?' she asked stiffly.

His mouth curved almost imperceptibly. 'Yes, it would. If we were eating there. But I thought it would be easier to have lunch here. We have a lot to discuss. This way we won't get interrupted.'

She couldn't stop her eyes from darting around the vast suite as her stomach gave a lurch that had nothing to do with hunger. Eat here. With Dante. *On her own.*

She cleared her throat, her body prickling with panic. 'That wasn't what we agreed.'

He was studying her face. 'You don't need to be scared of me, Talitha.'

'I'm not,' she said quickly—too quickly, she realised a moment later as the corners of his mouth tilted up fractionally.

'So, it's yourself you're afraid of?'

She felt the tension in her stomach wind tighter as

he walked towards her. 'I'm not going to dignify that with an answer,' she snapped as he stopped in front of her. 'I'm here to work.' She lifted her eyes challengingly. 'Unless, of course, you've changed your mind.'

'I haven't.' He gestured towards a table set for lunch. 'So perhaps we should sit down, and you can talk me through the process of building an art collection while we eat.'

She was still on edge, but it was easier, she found, to talk to him now she was following a script. And while they ate—a delicious herb-crusted rack of lamb, Jersey Royals, heritage carrots and pea purée—she explained everything from sourcing artworks and confirming authenticity and provenance to shipping and storage.

He asked a couple of questions but seemed distracted. His gaze kept drifting away from hers, and she was suddenly glad that lunch would soon be over. She didn't want to be reminded of how it felt to be not enough to hold his attention.

The waiter had returned with dessert. Or rather dessert for her. Glancing down at the plate, she felt herself blushing. It must just be a coincidence. Dante couldn't have remembered.

There was a beat of silence and, looking up, she felt the blood pulse through her body.

'*Budini di riso fiorentini.* With a coconut sorbet,' Dante said softly. 'I asked the kitchen to make it.'

He shifted back in his seat, and now she was the focus of his gaze. Her hand felt clumsy against her water glass. Beneath the sudden rapid beating of her heart she could hear the faint hum of traffic from the street outside and suddenly she was scared. Not of him, but of herself, and how vulnerable she still was to him. Only he must never guess…

The dessert was delicious. Soft and creamy but light, with a fresh citrus tang.

'Is a bespoke menu on offer to all the guests?' she asked crisply. 'Or does it only come with this particular suite?'

He didn't answer immediately. His eyes held hers, the grey of the irises dark and impenetrable like flint. 'No, it comes with being the owner of the hotel,' he said at last.

Her mouth didn't quite drop open, but she knew she might as well have had a speech bubble filled with exclamation marks coming out of the top of her head. 'This is your hotel?' She didn't recognise her voice. It sounded high and hoarse. 'I didn't know you owned a hotel.'

'Hotels. Plural.' He stared at her for a moment, and then added, 'I have many. Shall we take our coffee on the terrace? England has so little sunshine, it seems a shame to waste it.'

Before she had a chance to reply he stood up and walked across the suite to where sliding doors led onto a private balcony. Gritting her teeth, she followed him.

Wow, she thought silently, momentarily lost for words. It was like having your own exclusive viewing platform over London. She made no move to sit down in the L-shaped seating area, choosing instead to brace herself against the railing.

Having dismissed the waiter with a nod of his dark

head, Dante joined her. 'You seem surprised by my expansion into the hotel industry.'

She turned to face him, scowling. 'I thought crypto currency was your thing.'

He shrugged. 'It is. But I thought it wise to diversify, so as well as hotels I own other property, a film studio, and several newspapers. In fact, I have quite a few business interests in the UK, including—'

'Congratulations!' she interrupted him curtly. It was what he'd wanted when they were together. Money. Power. Prestige. Global domination.

Even in its embryonic stages it had consumed his life, their life together. But they weren't together now, and she didn't want to hear about the empire that he'd chosen over her.

'You must be very happy.'

He had picked up his cup and, taking a mouthful, he pulled a face. 'I would be if I could get a decent cup of coffee,' he said mildly. 'I need to speak to the kitchen about the beans we're using. This is too fruity, too acidic. A true espresso should be nutty, chocolatey, a little earthy. I think maybe I need to make a trip to Italy.'

She returned his gaze coldly. 'You should. And sooner rather than later.'

'I'm glad you think so.'

Something was happening. His eyes were fixed on hers as if he wanted to commit this moment to memory.

'I can't think why,' she said, not understanding but wanting to be free of the focus of his gaze. 'What you do and where you go has got nothing to do with me.'

She felt the tension throb between them in the silence that followed her words and suddenly she was holding her breath.

'Oh, but it has,' he said smoothly. 'I'm going to Italy and you're going to come with me. You're going to come and stay with me at my house in Siena.'

CHAPTER THREE

THIS TIME HER JAW did drop. Not just metaphorically but literally. She felt a lurch almost like vertigo.

Her heart was thumping hard against her chest, and the dampness of her hands had nothing to do with the sunlight beating on her back. If she hadn't been so appalled by his suggestion she might have laughed. Go with him to Italy? Stay in his home?

She stared at him in silence, momentarily deprived of speech by his spectacular disregard for her feelings and the absence of any emotion on his part.

'Are you out of your mind? No.' She shook her head emphatically. 'That's not going to happen.'

She didn't want to stay in his home as his employee. She didn't want to have breakfast with him in the mornings and dine with him in the evenings in some horrible parody of what their married life might have been like if he had meant the words of love he'd spoken to her in Milan.

It would be too painful.

Being so close, only not close at all...

She shook her head again. 'Working with you is bad

enough as it is. I am not going anywhere with you. And I am absolutely *not* going to be staying in your home.'

There was a long silence. Dante's gaze didn't flicker, but she saw a dangerous glitter in his dark eyes and she flattened her body against the railing, trying to create more distance between them as he took a step towards her.

His expression was serious, almost sombre. 'But earlier you said that the relationship of an artwork to its location requires careful consideration.'

Her fingers trembled against the railing and in that moment she hated him—hated how he could so effortlessly recall her words and use them against her.

'Actually,' he went on, staring at her as if he was testing her, 'you said that it was *crucial* to balance the works with their surroundings.' His expression was unreadable. 'And that it would require a site visit for you to fully understand the space.'

She dragged her gaze away from the glitter in his eyes.

She had said all those things.

Worse, she had been proud of her professionalism. But that had been when she had thought her part in this pantomime was almost over. It had never occurred to her that she would be the one doing a site visit.

And she wouldn't be.

Even if it meant losing this job.

'You're wasting your time, Dante.' Heart beating painfully fast, she lifted her chin. 'And don't think you can pull the *what-would-your-boss-think?* card this time,' she said bitterly. 'I'm done with being threatened by you.'

He was watching her steadily, his grey eyes cool, clinical, almost as if she was an exotic creature that he was studying.

'I'm not threatening you,' he said quietly. 'I don't need to. You will come to Italy, Talitha. In fact, you'll be eager to come,' he continued, his tone conversational. 'You see, as I tried to explain earlier, I have extensive business interests here in England.'

Her heart was banging uncomfortably against her ribs. What was that supposed to mean? And why did it sound like a threat?

Wishing she could read his thoughts, she stiffened her shoulders. 'You know, this international man of mystery routine is wearing a little thin, Dante.'

He was still staring at her in that same assessing way, infuriatingly calm in the face of her growing anger and frustration. Trying to calm herself, she reached out and picked up her coffee cup with a shaking hand.

She could feel something stirring in her. Only Dante had ever looked at her with such intensity. It was as if he was peeling back her skin, reaching inside her, claiming her. The hairs on the nape of her neck rose. How did he do it? And what was he thinking when he looked at her like that?

But she knew what he was thinking because she was thinking it too, and she knew that if she closed her eyes she would almost be able to feel the weight of his body overlapping hers.

His mouth.
His hands.
His—

Her belly clenched. Just remembering sent fluttering ripples of pleasure over her skin, so that for a moment she forgot where she was and why she was there. Breathing was an effort, thinking an impossibility. She was lost, swept away by the sudden heat in her veins and the slow, hypnotic pounding of her heart.

From somewhere down below a cacophony of car horns cut through her thundering heartbeat and, twisting her traitorous body away from the pull of his gaze, she said quickly, 'If you've got something to say, I suggest you stop speaking in riddles and just say it.'

He watched her: steady, patient, absolutely focused. He knew she was on edge. Knew that she was cornered.

'I'm a non-executive director for several companies,' he said finally. 'Including a private bank which I think might be of particular interest to you.'

The cup in her hand felt suddenly slippery and she put it down clumsily, slopping coffee into the saucer.

He waited a moment, and then he said quietly, 'Charles Tait is a good man.'

Slowly, like in those nightmares where your body refused to run from the monster, she stiffened her shoulders and forced herself to look him in the eye.

'How dare you? My account with Taits is private. You have no right—'

'I have every right.' His handsome face was impassive, but his voice crackled with authority. 'As do the other directors. Your debt is not some little bar tab, Talitha.'

His spare, brutal summing up of her finances made her flinch inside.

'Do you think I don't know that?' she snapped.

'So why haven't you dealt with it before now?'

A shiver raced through her as his face hardened.

'This isn't something you can just walk away from.' There was flint in his voice now. 'Your family owes a lot of money, and you have no way of paying it back—now or in the foreseeable future. Or did you think you could just toss that pretty little head of yours like a show pony and it would all just disappear?'

She passed a hand over her face, as if somehow that might brush his words away, and she heard him sigh.

'If it's any comfort, I didn't know you were a client when I accepted the position with Taits.'

It was no comfort. Her skin felt as if it was on fire. For months now she had been maintaining a perfect façade. It was all she had left. And that Dante, of all people, should know the truth made her feel sick.

'Why are you doing this?' Panic was rising inside her like a tidal wave, and despite all her efforts she couldn't stop her voice from shaking. 'Don't you think I've been punished enough?'

No, was the obvious answer to that question. But, watching Talitha wrap her arms around her body, Dante found himself hesitating. Wading through the St Croix Hamilton family's chaotic financial history with Taits, he had felt something pinch inside him. She was paying the price—metaphorically and literally—for her parents' incompetent and irresponsible spending habits.

But he refused to soften towards her. Talitha was hardly blameless. Up until last year she had never had to work for a living. Never had to lift a finger. She'd spent money like she did everything else—unthinkingly, and with the assumption that she deserved the best on offer.

His jaw tightened.

Talitha was spoiled and thoughtless and ruthlessly self-centred. She had used him and then discarded him.

She had no idea what it had taken for him to let down his guard. He had let her get closer than any other woman, trusted her more than any other woman, and what had she done but throw it all back in his face?

So *no*, to answer her question, she hadn't been punished enough.

But he was not about to reveal how badly she had hurt him.

He turned his head, letting his gaze drift across the London skyline. 'Actions have consequences, even for the St Croix Hamiltons of this world. Your family has been living on borrowed time. And borrowed money.'

The bank should have acted sooner—no doubt they would have done so with anyone else. His stomach twisted. But it was completely obvious that Charles Tait was smitten with Talitha.

'So you thought you'd put the clocks forward, did you?' Her voice was barely above a whisper. 'Hasten our demise? That's why you wanted this stupid meeting? To gloat?'

He dismissed her accusation with a careless lift of

his shoulders. 'I'm not here to gloat, Talitha. I'm here to discuss my art collection. But I'm happy to give you some independent advice, if you wish.'

'Advice?' She gave a humourless laugh. 'I don't need any advice from you. I know what I'm going to do.'

She didn't: he could hear the uncertainty weaving through her voice.

'I see. So you've decided to sell the estate?' he said smoothly.

'No. That's not going to happen.' There was a jagged edge to her voice. 'I'm going to sell the townhouse.'

God, she was stubborn, he thought, watching her. *And out of her depth.*

Even before he'd been able to talk, he had known that life was dog-eat-dog. It was hard and brutal and ugly. For a moment he stared past her, remembering the childhood he had discarded, the past he had buried beneath the lies he'd told himself and other people.

But what would she know of that? Living as she had with horses and cooks and gardeners, untouched by poverty and tragedy, never once thinking about the way other people clawed their way from one day to the next.

Glancing sideways, he studied her profile: the clean, curving jaw, the finely drawn arch of her eyebrows, the soft, pouting mouth. His gaze lingered on her mouth. Her lips were full, and painted a soft, dusky rose that he happened to know matched the colour of her nipples exactly.

He felt his groin grow hot and hard. Somewhere at the margins of his brain he could clearly see Talitha, naked on the bed in his apartment in Milan, her sun-saturated body arching up to meet his, her small, high breasts as warm and tempting as the white-fleshed peaches that they'd bought in the market and fed to each other in the bath.

Blanking his mind, he turned towards the cooling view of Hyde Park, where a few riders were trotting their ponies down the broad, sandy track of the Row. Nearby, he could see groups of Household Cavalry exercising their horses. There was a comforting order to the regimented progress of their blue and white jackets and distinctive jaunty red plumes.

'That won't be enough to satisfy the bank,' he said curtly, turning to face her. 'Surely Charles made that clear? Selling the estate is the only possible option available to you, and even then you'll probably still have to sell the townhouse too.'

She leaned forward, her eyes flashing with anger and frustration, and some other emotion he couldn't place. 'I'm not selling the estate.'

'It's just a house, Talitha. You can buy another one.'

'It's not just a house. Ashburnham has been in my family for generations. Selling it is not an option.'

His gaze shifted from her face to her tightly clenched fists, and the acid taste in his mouth burned all the way to his stomach. That was what mattered—what had always mattered most to her. Her estate. Her ancestry. Her name.

Not people.

And certainly not some nobody from a Naples slum.

'In that case, you might want to consider being a little more flexible,' he said coolly.

They gazed at one another, wary and unsmiling.

'What is this really about?' she asked at last.

Before he could stop it, he felt his body respond to her question. His gaze dropped to the tiny pulse beating frantically in her throat, and then lower still to the slim curves of her breasts beneath the yellow silk.

He shrugged. 'I told you. I want you to come to Siena.'

She raised her head. 'And I told you that's not going to happen.'

There was still a quiver of defiance in her face but the smudges under her eyes made her look young—too young to be dealing with a mess of this magnitude on her own. It wasn't as if she was some hotshot businesswoman—hell, she hadn't even had a job up until a few months ago. So where were the grown-ups? Her parents? Her grandfather?

'You don't know what I'm offering,' he said softly.

Leaning back against the railing, he watched a flush of colour spill across her cheeks.

'Whatever it is,' she said hoarsely, 'it could never be enough to tempt me into going anywhere with you.'

He put down his half-drunk cup of coffee. 'Really? Given your financial predicament, I would have thought you would be keen to clear your debts.'

She was staring at him blankly, her brown eyes wide with shock, or confusion, or maybe disbelief. 'What are you talking about?'

There was a silky sheen of perspiration above her upper lip and a few strands of hair had come loose from her ponytail. He had to tense the muscles in his arms to stop himself from reaching over and tucking them behind her ear.

'That's what I'm offering. You come to Siena and I will square your debt with the bank. Nobody will ever know how close you came to being another poor little ex-rich girl playing in the cinders. You get to keep the family seat and the St Croix Hamilton image intact— and I know how much having the perfect shopfront matters to people like you.'

There was a long, gritty silence. Her face was pale and still, like a stone statue, and he could see her mind racing, turning over his words, weighing them up, examining them.

'Why would you possibly want to do that?' she asked finally.

His gaze touched her blonde hair. He remembered what it felt like to wrap its glossy length around his hand, how he would tangle his fingers through it and pull back her head to expose the curve of her throat to his mouth.

That was why.

All week he had slept badly, his conversations with Talitha and Charlie replaying endlessly inside his head, blurring into one another.

Nothing he did seemed to make any difference.

Not even work.

His spine tensed. He'd had to force himself to concentrate. His mind had kept drifting off, only to make its way inevitably to Talitha, and then this morning he had woken and for the first time in days had felt clear-headed—almost as if he'd woken from some feverish dream.

He'd known what he needed to do to get her out of his head once and for all.

It was simple. He would make her come out to Italy and work for him. Give their relationship a distance and a formality that would override the frenzied passion of their short-lived affair and the pain of her betrayal.

Keeping his expression intentionally bland, he shrugged. 'Because I want you to curate my collection and that's what it will take to get what I want.'

The smudges under her eyes looked darker, but her gaze held his as she shook her head. 'So basically you're holding my home to ransom,' she said shakily. She shook her head. 'My answer is no.'

Of course it was, he thought, torn between exasperation and admiration. Most women in her position—most men—would be biting his hand off, but Talitha had a mile-wide streak of stubbornness equal only to his.

He shook his head. 'As usual, you're turning something simple and straightforward into a drama.'

She gave him an icy glare. 'You want simple and straightforward? Then how about goodbye? Or, better still, *ciao*?'

'*Ciao* also means hello, *ciccia*,' he said softly. 'Another reason for joining me in Siena. You get to practise your Italian.'

He felt lightheaded, but also exhilarated, like a diver on the Fiordo di Furore, looking down into the Tyrrhenian Sea.

'Unless, of course, it was a slip of the tongue.'

He watched her bite into her lower lip, suddenly aware of nothing beyond the beating of his heart and the darkening of her irises. As the silence between them lengthened, he felt the tension mount.

Finally, she blew out a breath. 'Look, Dante, me working for you, my loan from Taits—none of that changes the fact that I don't want to be a part of your life anymore. So why can't you stop trying to be a part of mine?'

He heard the flicker of emotion in her voice, the frustration, the conflict and the hunger. Could feel his own hunger pulsing in every cell in his body. His eyes locked with hers and then dropped to her mouth, lingering there before rising again to meet her gaze.

'I could, but it would inconvenience me to do so. I'm a very busy man, Talitha, and as you so rightly said, building an art collection requires a connection, an intimacy. We have that already, so why would I waste time recreating that with a third party?' He hesitated, letting his voice drop to a speculative murmur, 'Unless, of course, you still have feelings for me.'

'Feelings?' She took a step forward; she was trembling. 'I don't feel anything for you. Except an immense longing for you to disappear back under the stone you crawled out from. I mean, given what happened between us, what else could I be feeling?'

There was a beat of silence.

Afterwards, he tried to remember who made the first move. Perhaps he leaned into her, or perhaps she reached for him. But one moment they were standing opposite each other, not touching, and the next his hand was wrapped around her waist and Talitha was clutching his shirt as if it was a life jacket.

She took a quick breath like a gasp as his other hand found her face, his fingers moving gently across her cheek, tangling roughly through her hair so that it fell heavily to the base of her neck. He felt her mouth open under his and then she was kissing him back, the pale curve of her body swooning against his so that he could feel the taut tips of her nipples through his shirt.

He made a rough sound in his throat. His desire was raw. Unrestrained. Unthinking.

Behind him, the London skyline was moving in slow, tilting circles, like a huge panoramic kaleidoscope. Nothing had substance, nothing made sense—except Talitha and the wave of shivery pleasure building inside him.

His thighs moved between hers and heat exploded in his groin as she squirmed closer to where his erection was pressing against his trousers. Its hardness was too much to bear and he pulled her hips closer still. Lifting her hair from her neck, he found the pulse in the hollow beneath her ear, tracing its progress along her collarbone with his mouth. And then his hand moved up to the curve of her breast, his fingers sliding beneath the thin silk of her dress to find hot bare skin.

Her lips parted and she let out a low, scratchy moan…

What the hell was he doing?

Abruptly, he drew back, ignoring the protests of his body. Talitha was staring up at him, looking as dazed as he felt. Her face was flushed, her lips pink and swollen from his kisses, and she was trembling slightly. As if she'd been standing in the middle of a storm.

And she had been. They both had. A storm of passion.

Dizzily he braced himself against the railing, trying to quiet the chaos in his body. He hadn't lost control like that in years. Not since the first time he had set eyes on Talitha, in fact.

He felt his stomach clench. Ever since he'd walked out of Dubarry's he'd imagined kissing her—or rather he had thought about how he would look deep into her eyes, hold her close, and then show both of them that he was able to resist her.

It had all gone perfectly during the rehearsals inside his head, but when it had come to the actual performance he had weakened, her proximity lighting the touchpaper of his libido. His body had reacted to her as it had always done, so that he'd only had to touch her full, soft lips and he'd been drowning in pleasure.

Blanking his mind against how badly he wanted that pleasure to continue, he said coolly, 'I hope that answers your question.'

Her chin jerked upwards, almost as if he had slapped her, and just for a moment he wanted to take back his words. But then he remembered his silent apartment and the simple diamond engagement ring he'd given her sitting on the kitchen table, no longer a token of endless love but a wordless circle of rejection.

'My answer is the same,' she snapped. 'I'd rather clean toilets than be in debt to you.'

'So you don't need the money? You don't want to save your precious Ashburnham?'

Her face flushed. 'Not if it means doing a deal with the devil.'

'In that case,' he said softly, 'would you like me to put in a good word with Housekeeping? I'm sure they could find you some hours to suit.'

'Go back to hell, Dante,' she said tightly. Snatching up her bag, she spun round and stalked across the terrace. 'And this time,' she called over her shoulder, 'why don't you stay there?'

Stepping out of the shower, Talitha grabbed a towel and briskly rubbed her skin dry.

After leaving the Hanover she had called work and said that she had a migraine. She hated admitting to herself that Dante had got under her skin, but she had been too on edge to face everyone at the office. Too worried that they would somehow sense what had happened with him.

Or rather what she had allowed to happen with him.

She caught sight of her reflection in the mirror. She looked like she always did, so probably they wouldn't have noticed anything. But she felt different. Wound up. Jittery. *Ashamed.*

Her insides tightened. She should have stopped him. *Correction:* she should have stopped herself.

Because, much as she would like to blame Dante for what had happened on the terrace, deep down she knew that she had been as responsible as him for that kiss.

Only of course they'd had very different motives.

She had kissed him out of need, out of compulsion, meaning in that moment not to kiss him had been beyond her conscious control. But Dante had kissed her for the same reason he had broken off the kiss. To prove a point. To prove he could. To satisfy his curiosity and confirm what he had thought three years ago—that she was not enough to make him want more.

It had been a demonstration of power, not a helpless surrender to a desire that seemingly refused to die.

She grimaced and, seeking a moment of darkness and oblivion, closed her eyes. Instantly she could feel his mouth on hers, his fingers in her hair, his hand cupping her breast—

Her nipples tightened beneath the towel and her eyes snapped open. She banged her own hand against the side of the shower cubicle in frustration.

She was such an idiot.

How, after everything that she knew about him, could she have reacted as she had? But one touch was all it had taken for her to melt on the inside and into his arms. Even now, after she had spent half an hour washing every trace of him from her body, her skin was still prickling where he had touched it and she felt hot and restless and conflicted.

Somewhere in the house a clock chimed six and she bit her lip. She needed to dry her hair and change, otherwise she would be late. Stepping into her dressing room, she selected a simple cream dress, towel-dried her hair and smoothed it into a bun, and slipped her feet into a pair of low court shoes.

Gazing at her reflection, she breathed out shakily.

Like most people after a day at work, she would much rather throw on a pair of tracksuit bottoms or shorts and a T-shirt, but sticking to a routine and making as few unnecessary changes as possible was one of the things Dr Nolan had suggested to help keep her grandfather calm.

And Edward liked to dress for dinner and have a gin and tonic at six-thirty.

She felt a sudden stab of anger. Only what was the point of bringing her grandfather a gin and tonic every evening when she was going to be making him homeless any day now?

But of course Dr Nolan didn't know about that unwelcome but necessary change that was looming.

Her anger faded as she walked into the drawing room and caught sight of her grandfather. He was sitting outside on the terrace, his snowy hair just visible beneath his Panama hat, his head tilted towards the radio.

'Hi, Jill. How's he been today?' she said softly.

Jill was one of Edward's two live-in nurses. She worked alternate shifts with her colleague Michael. They were both specially trained in dementia care and had been looking after her grandfather for the last year and a half.

'He was good this morning. A bit confused this afternoon…you know, asking for your grandmother. But he's looking forward to his gin and tonic.'

She mixed the drink and made her way into the early evening sunlight.

'Hi, Grandpa.'

As Edward St Croix Hamilton looked up at her, she felt a tug on her heart. At eighty-one, he was still a handsome man, with fine features and the same clear brown eyes she met every day in the mirror, but there was a fragility to him now that had never been there before.

Leaning forward, she gently kissed the papery skin of his cheek. He smelled of the old-fashioned shaving soap he used and the cologne that her grandmother had always given him.

'Pamela?'

At the sound of her voice he looked up, smiling warmly and, swallowing past the lump in her throat, she crouched down beside him. 'No, Grandpa, it's me. Talitha.'

She made herself go on looking into his eyes, waiting, hoping that he would remember.

'Talitha...' He was staring at her as if he was seeing her through a fog.

'Yes, it's me, Grandpa. I've got your gin and tonic.'

'Is it that time already?'

She nodded, smiling. 'I made it just as you like it. Three to one ratio of tonic to gin. Lime, not lemon and plenty of ice.'

'Good girl. Just don't tell your grandmother.'

He looked so pleased with himself, like the man in his wedding photos, and, still smiling, she picked up his hand and squeezed it. Her grandmother had died nearly seventeen years ago, but that was another of Dr Nolan's rules. Avoid correcting the patient.

While he sipped his drink she read to him from his

newspaper, steering clear of the actual news and concentrating instead on the racing pages.

'It looks like Jimmy's got a runner in the two-thirty at Cheltenham,' she said, scanning the runners and riders for the next day's races. Jimmy Vincent was the son of her grandfather's former trainer, and fortunately he had the same name as his father, therefore avoiding any confusion in his mind. 'Would you like to have a little flutter?'

He didn't reply, and then she felt his hand squeeze hers.

'It's good of you to move back home, Talitha. I know you must miss your life in London.'

'Not at all,' she protested. 'I love Ashburnham. It's my home. Our home.' She glanced away to where a trio of fallow deer were cropping the grass beneath the spreading branches of a horse chestnut tree. 'It's so beautiful.'

'It is, isn't it?'

She turned back and felt her smile freeze. She stared at him, stricken. Tears were rolling down his cheeks.

'I don't think I could be happy anywhere else.' His face puckered. 'Promise me—promise me that we can stay here.'

Her chest hurt so badly it felt as if she had swallowed rocks. 'We're not going anywhere, Grandpa.' Her voice cracked a little and she cleared her throat. 'This will always be our home. I promise.'

They ate early, as usual, and she watched him carefully throughout the meal, keeping the conversation light and free-moving. To her relief he seemed to have completely forgotten his earlier distress.

But she hadn't forgotten.

And as soon as her grandfather was safely tucked up in bed she made her way to the library, pulled out her phone and, before she had a chance to change her mind, called the number that Harriet had given her for Dante.

She wasn't expecting to talk to him in person. Men like Dante didn't answer their phones. But that was fine. She would leave a message, and if necessary, she would go to the hotel and speak to him in person.

But she didn't have to do either of those things.

'Talitha.'

Around her the book-lined walls quivered, and hearing Dante say her name rendered her momentarily speechless, but then she remembered her grandfather's tears and, lifting her chin, took a deep breath.

'Is your offer still open?'

'It is. Have you changed your mind?'

He seemed utterly unfazed by her call, and for a moment she wavered.

'You will come to Italy,' he'd said. *'In fact, you'll be eager to come.'*

And now here she was, calling him back.

She swallowed past the panic building in her throat. He was always one step ahead of her. Still ruthless and single-mindedly pursuing his goals. And she was still hopelessly out of her depth.

But she had made a promise to her grandfather. And, unlike Dante King, she kept her promises. Going to his home, seeing the life he had built without her, might put an end to all the lingering regrets, the 'if onlys' that had stalked her for the last three years. Maybe then she would finally be free of the past.

'Yes, I have,' she said firmly. 'I've decided to come to Siena with you.'

There was a slight pause, and then he said quietly, 'I'll send a contract over.'

The line clicked as he hung up.

CHAPTER FOUR

PUSHING OPEN THE SHUTTERS, Talitha blinked dazedly into the early-morning Italian sunshine. She might have sold her soul to a devil, but it was her first morning in Tuscany and for a moment she forgot about everything that had happened over the last week and just enjoyed the view.

The sky was a brushstroke of brilliant endless blue, with not even a wisp of cloud in sight. The housekeeper, Angelica, had warned her that there would very likely be a *temporale* heading their way—but not today, she thought, glancing up at the sky again to where a bleached yellow sun hovered over the distant terracotta rooftops of Siena like a giant beach ball.

Up until that moment she had thought that nothing manmade could compete with the beauty of a perfect summer's day. But she'd been wrong.

Her gaze dropped down to the wisteria-covered walkways meandering between box-edged geometric beds of lilies and irises and the pergolas swathed in climbing roses. Over a dusky-pink brick wall the geometric precision softened into meadows of wildflowers, stretching out to a gleaming mass of water fringed by a forest of trees, and then onwards to khaki-coloured olive groves and vineyards.

It was a glorious view and, according to Angelica, all of it belonged to Dante.

She blew out a breath. If only she was here on holiday. She would love to mooch around the gardens and then take a trip into Siena and wander the medieval streets like an ordinary tourist. But she wasn't here to wander, and she certainly wouldn't be doing any sightseeing. She was here to work.

When that was done, she would go back to her life in England. Not the same life, though. She wanted to make a few changes. Sell the townhouse. Talk to Philip about her future.

One thing was certain. There would be no more jumping through hoops for Dante King. In fact, hopefully this would be the last time she ever had to see him.

Assuming she did actually see him.

She felt a beat of anger pulse across her skin. If she had needed proof that she was right about the man she had come so close to marrying then she had it now. It was typical of Dante, she thought irritably. He had been the one pushing to make this happen. And here she was, in his beautiful seventeenth-century Baroque home. Only the man himself was nowhere to be seen.

Pulse accelerating, she watched a lean black cat stalk a pale lilac petal across the terrace.

It was different from when they'd been in Milan. Then she had loved him so much that whenever he'd taken his hands off her she'd felt his absence like an actual physical emptiness, as though someone had scooped out her insides. Now her pride was the only casualty; she had a niggling sense that she was being played with like a puppet.

Her mouth thinned. They were in different places, and both of them were different people now, but one thing hadn't changed. She was still marking time, waiting for him to return.

The steward had been apologetic as she'd stepped into Dante's private jet. Signor King was very sorry, he said, to miss the opportunity of accompanying Signorina Hamilton on the flight, but he had been unavoidably delayed.

It had taken several seconds for the full implication of his words to register, and when they had any lingering doubts as to where she stood and why he had kissed her had been instantly resolved.

She had been right: that kiss had had nothing to do with passion. It had been about putting her in her place, having the last word.

Cheeks flaming, she remembered how eagerly she had pulled his hard body against hers. How for those few frenzied seconds she had imagined it was real.

It was maddeningly frustrating—not to say humiliating—to find out all these years later that her attraction to him hadn't become any less. But in a way wasn't it a good thing? Knowing that he was prepared to ruthlessly manipulate the chemistry they'd once shared would surely make it so much easier to keep her wayward physical response to him in check?

And she clearly needed all the help she could get.

She showered quickly, leaving her hair loose to air-dry, and then stared at her clothes, a prickle of resentment spreading over her skin. She would have much preferred to wear something casual, but after what had happened on the terrace at the Hanover she wanted to make it clear that she was here to work, so she had packed accordingly.

Only it was so hot.

In the end she chose a pair of navy tailored Bermuda shorts with a pale pink wrap blouse and tan-coloured gladiator sandals. She always wore the watch her grandfather had given her for her twenty-first birthday, but she wore no other jewellery aside from two pearl studs that showed when her hair fell away from her ears.

As she made her way downstairs, she felt her nerves dance back to life. It was just four days since she'd called Dante and told him she'd changed her mind, and she still couldn't quite believe that she was here. Everything had been arranged with head-spinning swiftness.

After finally agreeing to Dante's request, she had been slightly anxious that Philip might veto the trip on such short notice, but her boss had practically purred with joy when he'd heard that she was doing a site visit. A site visit meant the client was serious. More importantly, it meant he was going to spend serious money.

Telling her grandfather that she was going to be away for a few days had made her anxious for different reasons. Fortunately, she'd caught him on one of his good days. He had taken it well, and she had left strict instructions for Jill and Michael to call her if anything happened.

And of course there had been none of the usual fussing around flights or hotels.

A pulse skimmed across her skin as she made her way downstairs. She had been on private jets in the years before Dante. But it felt like a lifetime ago now. Back then she had been footloose and fancy-free; utterly and blissfully unaware of the true cost of anything.

She felt her stomach twist.

Was there a price for relinquishing your pride? If so, then she was paying it. But she would willingly pay any price to make sure her grandfather was safe and happy, and that was why, in the end, she had agreed to come here. To keep the wolf from the door.

Picturing Dante's handsome face, his grey eyes narrowed on hers, she felt her heart begin to thud rhythmically. Keeping the wolf from the door was all well and good when you were in your own home, but right now she was in Dante's. And how could she keep the wolf from the door when she was living under his roof?

'*Buongiorno*, Signorina Hamilton.'

Angelica greeted her warmly as she reached the bottom of the stairs.

'I hope the bed was comfortable, and that you slept well, *signorina*.'

'Yes, thank you,' she lied.

Dante might not have been in the house, but he had roamed her dreams freely, his face drifting unchallenged through her subconscious, and she had woken at one o'clock, then three, tangled in the sheets, her body twitching restlessly.

But obviously she wasn't going to tell the housekeeper that. Angelica had done everything possible to make her feel welcome, and it wasn't her fault that her boss had been put on earth to torment Talitha.

'I thought you would like to breakfast on the terrace.'

Talitha smiled. 'That would be lovely,' she said truthfully.

Breakfast lately had been a snatched piece of toast and then a take-out coffee when she got to work. Breakfast Villa Bencivenni-style was a little more elaborate. *Bomboloni* filled with *crema*, sticky, flaky, caramelised *sfoglie*, apricot jam *crostata*, cut into large squares, powdery *millefoglie*...

'You don't like it?' Angelica was staring at her with concern. 'I can have Antonio do pancetta with some eggs, if you prefer.'

'No, this is perfect,' she said quickly. 'I'm just trying to make up my mind.'

In the end, she chose a *cornetto integrale* with a *caffè* latte. The pastry was delicious, sweeter and softer than its French counterpart, but it was the coffee that most surprised her. It was nutty, with a dark, caramel sweetness, and after one mouthful she found herself reluctantly agreeing with Dante.

She could have sat there all morning, just drinking coffee and gazing at the mesmerising view, and once again she found herself wishing she was simply on holiday. But the sooner this was done, the quicker she could go home.

Wandering through the house, she felt her heart lurch.

So this was what Dante had been chasing all those years ago. This, not a life with her, had been his goal.

Having grown up at Ashburnham, she was used to elegance and tradition—and, despite the paint flaking off the window frames and the dust motes spiralling up to the ceilings, her home still had a tarnished grandeur.

But even when Ashburnham was picture-perfect, it would be no competition for the Villa Bencivenni's palatial opulence.

The walls were mostly bare, but there was a museum-worthy collection of Murano glassware, Foggini chandeliers and Limoges porcelain. And with its gallery-sized rooms, and soft, natural light filtering through the deep-set windows the villa was a gift for any curator, so that despite her irritation with Dante she felt a quivering excitement skate across her skin.

There was a Francis Bacon that would sing in the exquisite cream-coloured drawing room, and she had the perfect Ellsworth Kelly diptych in mind for the incredible dining room, with its vast vaulted ceiling.

She scowled at a priceless bronze figurine of Amitayus, sitting serene and oblivious on an antique walnut credenza. Obviously she would need to run all that past Dante when—*if*—he ever decided to turn up.

After a quick lunch break she got straight back to work and, despite her reservations about coming to Italy, she couldn't deny that it had been worthwhile.

But by the middle of the afternoon she found herself wandering from room to room and then out onto the terrace, twitching with frustration.

Dropping down into one of the teak armchairs, she stared across the beautiful gardens, trying to ease the stabbing tension between her shoulder blades. This was supposed to be a collaborative process—a curator was as much a sparring partner as an advisor—only with Dante absent she couldn't spar on her own. And all this waiting around was giving her flashbacks to Milan.

'Having fun?'

The deep, masculine voice took her by surprise and she froze, her eyes narrowing on the man silhouetted in the doorway. The silhouette lingered for a moment and then Dante stepped into the light. In his dark suit, crisp white shirt, knitted tie and black leather shoes, he looked utterly out of place among the soft green foliage and bright sunlight.

She blinked. 'I didn't know you'd arrived.'

For a moment his slate-coloured eyes locked with hers. 'Evidently,' he said coolly. 'Why else would you be out here topping up your tan instead of doing what you're being paid to do?'

Watching a flush of pink spread across Talitha's cheeks, Dante felt anger flare beneath his skin. Arriving at the villa, he'd assumed he would find her working, or at least dressed for work. But here she was, wearing some whimsical pink confection and shorts that showed off her long, lightly tanned legs, with her blonde hair loose and spilling over her shoulders.

But should he really be surprised?

A work ethic was simply not part of her DNA.

His shoulders tensed. It was not part of his DNA either, but that was where the similarities between him and Talitha began and ended.

She had nothing to prove, nothing to outrun. On the contrary, her name had gifted her a Sybaritic life among the gods. Thanks to his name—his *real* name—people had judged him from birth, applied a label and then turned their backs on him.

Not that Talitha had needed that knowledge as an excuse to turn away.

He felt his stomach clench, remembering how close he had come to telling her the truth about his childhood, about his family.

He was lucky; he had been given a way out. But he had known right from the start that he couldn't rely forever on luck to stop him from being pulled back into that world. Luck was too fickle, too random. He needed something he could rely on. Something that would mean nobody would ever connect him with the baby born in a prison cell in Naples.

And that was why he worked and why he would keep on working. Not for money, but for what money could buy. He was rewriting his DNA, erasing the past, defying the legacy of his family, one penthouse and one private jet at a time.

It was a long journey, but he had only strayed from his path once. When he'd met the woman standing in front of him now, and had stupidly thought he could have it all.

Thanks to her, he knew that wasn't possible.

'I was working,' she snapped. 'I've been working all day. I was just taking a break.' Her eyes narrowed. 'But it would be difficult for me to do much more than I have without the client present. That's you, by the way, in case you've forgotten.'

Ignoring the sarcasm in her voice, he shrugged. 'I have offices all over the world. That means a twenty-four-hour working day. Something came up.'

That was a lie. The truth was that he had deliberately chosen not to fly with her. After what had happened in his suite, spending two hours with Talitha in a confined space had seemed like the very definition of a bad idea.

Not that he was worried it would happen again. But he'd been more shaken than he cared to admit by the kiss they'd shared.

By how it felt to have her in his arms again.

His pulse beat a little faster. After she'd stormed out he'd been furious with himself. He had lost control *again*, and in a few frenzied, mindless minutes undone three years' worth of the effort he'd made trying to forget her.

She had tasted so sweet. The temptation to give himself up to her sweetness had been almost more than he'd been able to bear...

And that was the worst part.

He should find it easy not to want her. After all, he knew her. He knew what she was like. Talitha had used him, then left him—not high and dry, but drowning in disbelief and despair. How could he know all that, and feel this angry, and yet still be so physically drawn to her?

'You don't need to tell me how busy you are, Dante,' she said crisply. 'Or remind me that with you business always comes first.'

His jaw tightened. It had been her constant complaint in Milan. That he had to work, that he wouldn't play hooky. Although he had, on more than one occasion, and each time it had physically hurt to pull his body away from hers and return to the office.

Remembering those stolen hours in his apartment, he felt his groin harden. They'd had sex on the bed and in the shower, on the floor and even out on the balcony. But it had been more than just bodies moving. It had been transformative. He had lost himself in her, and for the first time in his life he had forgotten who and what he was.

Talitha chose that moment to lean forward and brush a petal off her ankle. The movement made the neckline of her blouse gape invitingly away from her skin and his breathing jerked as he caught a glimpse of her breast and a soft, rosy nipple.

Gritting his teeth, he brought his mind back to the matter in hand. 'You appear to be a little confused, Talitha,' he said curtly. 'I'm not just buying pretty pictures to hang on my walls. For me, this is business. It's an investment, exactly like any other, and as with any other investment I'm looking to make a profit. It just so happens that on this occasion I'm investing in culture, not condos.'

'Art is nothing like a condo,' she protested. 'It's a

creative vision. Art defines beauty. It can be provocative and confrontational or stimulating and desirable. A condo can't do that.'

No, it couldn't, he thought, unable to look away from the fire in her eyes. But none of that mattered. Nor did making a profit. No, the reason he wanted an art collection was, ironically, down to Talitha.

It had been a hot day, and he had been trying to finish off some work at home, but Talitha had had other ideas. Pulling off her clothes, she had turned off his computer and climbed onto his lap.

'Nobody should work on a day like this, Dante. Just buy a painting instead.'

She had pressed her hand flat against the swell of his erection.

'Trust me. I know what I'm talking about. Art is worth more than you pay for it. It rises above money and makes people look at you with respect,' she'd said, between kisses.

She was right. Owning art put you on a different level. It put you out of reach, cloaking you with a kind of protective colouring. A bit like the 'razzle dazzle' camouflage used on warships in the Second World War.

He shook his head. 'Art is money on a wall.'

Her chin lifted. 'Not everything in life is about money, Dante.'

His eyes held hers. 'Easy to say when someone else is paying the bills,' he said softly.

Two stripes of colour flared along her cheekbones.

For a moment the only sounds were the faint splashes of water off stone from a nearby fountain.

'Then I suggest we get back to work, Mr King,' she said at last. She gave him a haughty stare. 'After all, time is money. *Your* money.'

Seriously?

It was that snooty little stare that did it. How could she look down her nose at him when it was his money that was getting her off the hook with the bank? This was the Talitha he knew, he thought savagely. The entitled little rich girl used to bewitching every hapless man who crossed her path, greedily helping herself to jobs and bank loans as if they were sweeties, with never a thought of lifting a finger in return.

Only she wasn't rich anymore.

He took a step towards her, holding on to his temper by a hair-fine thread. He kept talking about being in charge—perhaps he should behave as if he was.

'Don't push it, *ciccia*. You might be able to twist every other man with a pulse around your little finger, but I'm not like every other man. There's going to be no more favours, no more special treatment. If you want to keep your house then we're going to do things my way. Are you listening? Am I making myself clear?'

He snapped his fingers in front of her face, and as her eyes flew to his he felt a rush of satisfaction. This was why she was here. So that he could redress the balance of their relationship. See her in her true colours rather than through the distorting lens of her sensuality. Then, finally, he would get her out of his system.

She stared at him as if he was something she needed to wipe off her shoe. 'As crystal,' she said stiffly.

The rest of the day was one of the least satisfactory he had ever spent 'working'.

They sat at right angles to one another in the drawing room, their knees practically touching, but Talitha barely acknowledged his presence. Aside from when she was talking about specific works of art she spoke almost entirely in monosyllables, even during lunch.

The only time her frostiness thawed was when Angelica came into the room. Then he had to endure the sight of her blessing his housekeeper with one of her dazzling, irresistible smiles. But other than that her nose was glued to her laptop.

Surprisingly, this didn't please him as much as it should have done. More surprisingly still, he realised that she had been telling the truth when she'd said that she was good at her job.

As he'd suspected, she hadn't had an interview for her position at Dubarry's—not a formal one anyway. He'd learned that the other day, when Philip Dubarry had let slip that he was a friend of her family. But she was exceptionally well-informed, focused, and passionate about art. Far more so than the average pretty rich girl who had studied history of art at the Courtauld.

He wondered how and when she had picked up her knowledge. Back in Milan they had never talked much. Or rather *he* had never talked. Talitha had talked all the time, but not about anything like art. Mostly it had been about what she had done during the day and the people she knew. She'd seemed to live entirely in the present, with no plans for the future and no apparent interest in the past, and that had suited him fine.

It had more than suited him. He'd been captivated by her.

Afterwards, when it had all fallen apart, he had characterised her as careless. A beautiful, fickle child who needed constant entertainment, playing with things until she got bored and then smashing them and retreating behind her money.

But it appeared there was more to Talitha than he'd suspected.

'I like this Kiefer.' He twisted his laptop around to face her. 'But I also like this Freud. Do you have an opinion on which would work best in here?'

She glanced up at his screen, her mouth forming a pout. 'The Freud,' she said tersely.

'I prefer the Kiefer.'

'Okay,' she said tonelessly.

He shifted back in his seat, his eyes lingering on her pouting lips. 'Why shouldn't I choose the Kiefer?'

Her eyes didn't budge from her laptop. 'The Freud is a known commodity. Financially it's a less risky purchase.'

'But if you took money out of the equation?'

Now she lifted her chin, taking the bait as he had known she would. 'You can't,' she said sweetly. 'Art is just money on a wall.'

He let a beat of silence bounce between them.

'It's also a creative vision that defines beauty,' he

said softly. 'Art can be provocative and confrontational or stimulating and desirable.'

A bit like Talitha herself, he thought, as she stared up at him warily.

'That's my opinion, not yours.'

Their eyes locked. 'So change my mind. I want you to change my mind.'

She licked her lips and her pupils flared, the black swallowing up the brown, and he felt a swooping, vertiginous rush of desire as she seemed to sway towards him. This close to her, he was intensely aware of the light floral perfume she'd worn in Milan, and he could feel his body reacting viscerally, hungrily, to the memory of how he'd loved to slowly peel off her clothes and inhale her scent. All of her scents.

A shadow crossed in front of the window: his gardener, Mauro.

'That's not my job.' Blinking, she sat up straighter.

'You're here to guide me.'

'Yes, but you've made your motivation clear. You want investment pieces. Reliable heavyweights.' There was a sharp-edged, brittle tension to her voice. 'You're risk-averse.'

'Not true. I'm happy to take risks. I just don't like being played for a fool.'

Her eyes narrowed. 'You're many things, Dante, but a fool isn't one of them.'

He stared at her in silence. He'd been a fool for her. Tongue-tied, dazed. More like a stuttering adolescent than a man. Was that why she had walked away? Or had she never meant it to last?

'Why didn't you marry Ned Forester?'

As she looked up at him, her eyes widening with shock, he felt his heart beat a little faster as he realised that he had spoken out loud. But, dammit, why shouldn't he ask?

She stiffened 'I don't—I don't want to talk about that.'

Misery wrapped around his throat. In other words, she had been in love with another man the entire time she'd been with him.

'Tough. Because I do,' he said. The edge in his voice was an unmistakable reminder that he was calling the shots. 'And I think you owe me that.'

Talitha stared at him, her heart pounding so hard that it hurt. '*Owe* you?' she echoed. Did he think that by clearing her debt he somehow owned her, body and soul?

She thought back to that treacherous chasm of lost time a moment ago when he had stared so deeply into her eyes that she had forgotten to breathe, and her thoughts had lost shape, and her pulse had been drumming hard for danger. They had been seconds away from kissing again. Truthfully, she might be still vulnerable where her body was concerned, but her soul was strictly off-limits.

'I don't owe you anything, Dante.'

Her skin was prickling. Just seconds earlier she had actually thought he was taking her seriously, and that they might be able to work together. She'd even thought he might have drawn a line under their relationship and was starting to see her as an okay person.

She swallowed, not wanting to dwell on her stupidity. 'We have an agreement, and I am here now fulfilling the terms of that agreement.'

'Did he ask you to marry him again? Or did you ask him?' he went on remorselessly, as if she hadn't spoken. 'Did you break it off? Or did he? Did—?'

'Stop! Just stop it, Dante.' She slammed her laptop shut. 'He asked me. I bumped into him when I got back from Milan and we saw each other a couple of times.'

His jaw tightened. 'You mean you slept with each other.'

It was a statement, not a question, and she felt a rush of anger. 'No, I didn't sleep with him. I haven't slept with anyone since you.'

Dante was staring at her as if he didn't recognise her. 'I don't believe you.'

'I don't care,' she snapped. 'I'm not here to change your mind, Dante. I'm just telling you the facts.'

'And according to those facts he was your boyfriend.'

'No! We met up maybe three times as friends,' she corrected him. 'It wasn't romantic. Not for me, anyway,' she admitted. 'And I truly thought Ned felt the same way. But he didn't, and he asked me to marry him again, and…' she swallowed '…and this time I said yes.'

'I thought you were just friends.'

Her heart thudded heavily in her chest as his eyes slammed into hers. 'We were.'

'So, what? You needed a little ego-boost?'

The cool disdain in his voice made her skin sting.

What she had wanted was a shoulder to cry on, but then Ned had been so sweet, and just for a moment she had weakened.

She gave a slight shake of her head. 'It wasn't like that. I knew I didn't love him, and that I didn't want to marry him, and I should have told him immediately.'

'And yet you didn't.'

She felt his narrowed gaze on her face.

'Strange. I would have thought it would be easier the second time around. I mean, you'd already had practice in telling a man you didn't love that you didn't want to marry him.'

Her heart twisted. *Was that what he thought? Hadn't he known how much she loved him?*

She almost asked him that exact question—but what was the point? It was too late. They'd moved past a time when it could have made a difference.

'Something happened and…' She faltered, remembering the phone call, her grandfather's panicky voice. 'Something came up and I didn't have a chance to speak to him. By the time I did, he'd already told a few people.'

For a moment she thought about telling him the truth. Every detail. From how her father had squandered the family money to her grandfather's dementia. But thanks to his role at Taits he already knew way more than she wanted him to know about her private life.

'Why does any of this matter anyway?' she asked, lifting her chin, anger splicing through her.

Why did he get to push her on this? And what about

the part he'd played in the disintegration of their relationship? Suddenly she wanted to hit him—hurt him
as much as he had hurt her and was still hurting her.

'We'd split up by then. But I suppose you don't want
to talk about that.'

His eyes held hers, narrow, dark, challenging. 'Do
you want to talk about that?'

Her stomach clenched. Maybe for a short time he'd
thought himself in love with her, but she knew he
hadn't loved her in a swooning, always and for ever
kind of way. She had known that the moment he'd told
her he was going to visit his parents on his own, had
understood then that he wasn't serious.

But did she want him to say it to her face?

She was suddenly shaking inside. Even the idea of
it made her feel sick.

Feigning indifference, she shook her head. 'No, I
don't.' She waited a beat and then, avoiding his eyes,
opened her laptop.

Work was her ticket out of here, and right now that
was the only thing she truly wanted. To go home.
Her fingers stilled against the keyboard. In the mean-
time, she was just going to have to find a way to get
through the next few days without either kissing or
killing Dante.

CHAPTER FIVE

'Talitha, have you had a good day?'

Hearing her grandfather's voice, Talitha squeezed the phone tighter and for the first time since arriving in Siena felt her body relax.

She dropped down into one of the linen-covered armchairs by the window. Thankfully, after their confrontation in the drawing room, Dante had retreated to his study. She had spent the rest of the afternoon on the phone, negotiating a price for the Kiefer and the Freud he'd selected.

Ordinarily that would be a cause for celebration, but when he'd finally emerged for supper he had simply nodded. She had half expected him to start interrogating her again, but they'd eaten in near silence and the meal had been over within an hour. Afterwards he had returned to his study, and she'd scampered upstairs— to 'decompress', as Philip liked to say, when he came back from seeing a particularly challenging client.

It was still early, and in a parallel universe she might have stretched out on the exquisite pink velvet chaise-longue and read a book, or simply stared at the view.

But after the day she'd had she wanted, *needed* to remind herself why she was putting herself through all of this.

'It's been wonderful, Grandpa,' she lied. 'The weather's perfect and I had the most delicious mushroom *cappelletti* for supper tonight.'

That, at least, was true. From the starter of pan-fried scallops on a pea cream to the delicately flavoured coffee mousse for dessert, the food had been mouthwateringly good.

'And when will you be home?'

There was an anxious note in his voice now and she felt a buzz of panic in her bones. Had he forgotten she was in Italy?

'Soon,' she said carefully. 'But I need to finish this job in Siena. For Philip.'

She could picture her grandfather's face, the crease in his forehead as his ravaged brain tried to make sense of her words.

'Yes, I remember now,' he said more firmly. 'But you must have free time, so tell me, have you been to the Duomo?'

'Not yet, Grandpa.' With relief, she let out the breath she'd been holding. 'I've only been here a day.'

'But you must go, Talitha. It's dazzling. A triumph of Romanesque-Gothic architecture…'

Tucking her legs to the side, she leaned back and let him tell her about the intricate white, green and red marble façade of the Duomo, its elaborate Nicola Pisano pulpit and the sculptures by Michelangelo, Donatello and Bernini.

Sometimes when he was like this, so calm and so lucid, she could forget that he had Alzheimer's. But she knew that, in the early stages at least, memory problems were intermittent, and Dr Nolan had warned her that as the illness progressed he would get more confused and start to have increasing trouble organising his thoughts.

And that was only the beginning. In the future he might experience a change in personality and struggle to recognise friends and family members. There were drugs that could help, but at the moment there was no cure, and his deterioration was inevitable. The only question was over the speed at which he'd decline.

All she could do was make his daily life as comfortable and steady as possible. Having a routine and familiar things around him would help him to feel secure. In other words, he needed to keep on living at Ashburnham, and now thankfully that was possible.

If she did nothing else in her life she could be proud of that, she thought, her throat tightening a little as she said goodbye.

By the time she had written up her notes the sky was turning a deeper shade of blue at the horizon and a pale, pearlescent moon had finally ousted the sun. Reaching under her pillow, she pulled out her pyjamas. She had bought them specifically for the trip and they were perfect.

By 'perfect' she meant boyish and practical. In other words, nothing like the wisps of lace-edged silk and tulle she'd worn the last time she was in Italy.

With Dante.

And just like that, almost as if he had been waiting in the wings, Dante was inside her head and she could see him lying on the bed, his arm folded behind his head, those bewitching grey eyes soft and hazy with desire, his beautiful golden body stretched out like a dozing lion against the tangled sheets.

She pressed her hand across her mouth, felt her breath damp and shaky against her fingers. She had promised herself that she wouldn't think about him here in her room and she had been doing just fine.

But she was in Dante's house, so of course it was impossible to escape. Even inside her head.

Especially inside her head.

Her mind clicked slowly through the day: his sudden appearance in the garden, the near silent lunch, and then that interrogation in the drawing room followed by a near silent supper.

And don't forget that moment when you almost kissed again, an accusing little voice whispered in her ear.

She turned and walked swiftly across the room towards the open window, as if by doing so she could somehow outrun the memory of that moment.

But who was she trying to kid? She would have more luck evicting Dante from his home. And as for thinking that a pair of pyjamas could somehow neutralise the fact that he was sleeping under the same roof as she was—

Her eyes narrowed.

Except that he wasn't sleeping.

Or not at this moment in time anyhow.

She edged behind the filmy muslin curtains and stared down into the garden. A figure was silhouetted against the pale stone balustrade, head bowed, walking slowly back and forth across the flagstones.

As if sensing her gaze, Dante glanced up at the window and she shrank back into the shadows. For a second she almost felt as if she was floating. She couldn't feel her limbs, and the breath seemed to have left her body. Then he turned and walked in the opposite direction, and she exhaled shakily.

It must be nearly one in the morning. So what was he doing? Her lip curled. Given that he was still dressed in his suit, minus the tie, probably working. More master of the universe stuff, she thought irritably.

Heart thumping against her ribs, she watched as he stepped off the terrace and walked down one of the paths. Only he didn't look like a man straddling the world like a colossus. On the contrary, he looked more like Atlas.

There was something oddly vulnerable about the set of his shoulders, and she wondered why it seemed so familiar.

And then with a jolt she remembered.

It had been after her grandmother's funeral. All the guests had gone home, and she'd been supposed to be in bed—only she hadn't been able to sleep and she had crept downstairs. Her grandfather had been sitting, not standing, on the terrace, his head bowed as if an immense burden was crushing him.

Her heart pulsed in her throat.

But her grandfather had been hurting. He had just

lost his wife of forty years. His only son had abandoned not just his family but his duties, disappearing off to the Caribbean to fritter away the Hamilton fortune.

Dante had an enviable life. *Didn't he?*

There was only one person who could answer that, but even if she had been in a position to ask him she had learned from experience that direct questions were not a hugely successful method of eliciting information from Dante.

Watching him turn again and pace back along the path, she nibbled her thumbnail. She'd been so caught up with hating him, and then with trying to quell her attraction to him, that she had forgotten he was a person.

But Dante was nothing like her grandfather, and thinking about him in that way wasn't clever. The last thing she needed was a reason to care about him. Besides, it was none of her business, she told herself as Dante was swallowed by the darkness. Not anymore. Not ever again.

Rolling over onto his side, Dante reached out and fumbled on the table beside his bed for his watch. He squinted at the face and then his eyes widened with shock.

Surely it couldn't be that time! He never slept this late.

Throwing back the covers, he stood up and stalked across the room to the bathroom and into the shower, seething with frustration.

As the cool water hit his skin, he flinched.

Back in London, when fate had thrown them together, he had been forced to acknowledge that he and Talitha had loose ends to tie up. Bringing her out here, forcing her to be at his beck and call had seemed like an appropriate punishment for what she'd done, and he'd been looking forward to making her squirm.

Now, though, he was starting to think that he had made a catastrophic error of judgement.

His mouth twisted. It wouldn't be the first time where Talitha was concerned.

Slamming off the water, he snatched a towel, drying himself as he walked into his dressing room. He pulled open a drawer with unnecessary force, and as it sprung out it caught his knuckle.

'Porca puttana!' He slammed it shut.

He had wanted to turn the tables on her, prove to himself, and to her, that this time he was calling the shots. And theoretically he was.

Except if he was in charge then how come he kept losing control?

First at the Hanover and then again in the drawing room. Both times he had been pulled into a twisting tornado of emotion, his anger and frustration and desire whipping at his senses so that he hadn't known left from right or up from down.

This unwelcome and ungovernable explosion of emotion was not part of the plan. Nor was having sex with Talitha.

So why was it all he could think about?

He stared blankly at the rows of handmade suits and shirts, his temper fizzing. After supper he had shut himself in his study and tried to blot out the day, but each time he'd stared down at the screen of his laptop he had seen Talitha's face.

Everything she did and said seemed designed to confound and contradict what he believed to be true about her. Like when she'd told him she hadn't slept with anyone else. Of course, she had to be lying. Although she had no reason to.

He swore under his breath.

He was doing it again. Letting her get inside his head. Just as he had done last night, so that it had been the early hours of the morning before exhaustion had brought him a few hours of oblivion. And now he was running an hour late.

Grabbing a pair of chinos and a polo shirt, he dressed in minutes and made his way downstairs.

It was his own fault. Bringing her here had been a spur-of-the-moment decision and he didn't do those. They were too high risk and, as Talitha said, he was risk-averse. And as for picking over the bones of their relationship—

He gritted his teeth. No good ever came from revisiting the past—he knew that. In fact, putting as much distance between himself and his childhood had been the driving force of his life. And yet with Talitha he just couldn't seem to stop himself. He was like a child picking at a scab.

Maybe it was because she so obviously didn't want to talk about it. His chest tightened. For the equally obvious reason that he'd been in the right and she in the wrong.

'*Buongiorno*, Angelica. Just a coffee, please,' he said, stepping out onto the terrace.

Outside of the house's thick walls the air was heavy with heat and scent, so that it was almost like walking into a perfumed sauna. He stared upwards assessingly, shielding his eyes from the sun. There were no clouds, but the sky was a different kind of blue today and he could feel it—in fact he was certain of it. A storm was on its way.

'Looks like we're going to see some rain,' he said.

'*Si*, Signor King. There is so much tension right now. It is impossible to think, to go about one's business. Soon it will be too much, and it will snap, and then it will be better.'

Glancing over to where his housekeeper was innocently pouring his coffee, Dante felt his skin tighten. Was she still talking about the weather?

A pulse beating across his skin, he turned and, gazing across the empty terrace, said casually, 'Angelica, have you seen Ms Hamilton at all this morning?'

Handing him his coffee, Angelica nodded. '*Si, signor.* She was up very early. She asked to see the original plans of the garden. And then I think she went to look at *il tempio di Diana.*' His housekeeper frowned. 'She was most excited when I told her that the statue was missing.'

Now it was his turn to frown. And as Angelica disappeared back inside the house he felt a tug of curiosity. Why would anyone be excited by that?

Heartbeat accelerating, he put down his untouched coffee, and before he realised what he was doing he was walking away from the house towards a just visible patch of shimmering water.

It was a thirty-minute walk to the ornamental lake.

He got there in twenty.

He loved everything about his home, but the lake was not only his favourite place on the estate, it was probably his favourite place in the world. Here more than anywhere he felt safe...out of reach.

In truth, it was more of a pond than a lake. Shallow enough for a person to stand up in most places, it was edged by weeping willows and alders, and its smooth surface was stippled with water lilies. At its centre was an island, and in the middle of the island was a colonnaded temple—*il tempio di Diana*.

Diana herself had gone missing—stolen many years ago.

His breath caught in his throat. But today it seemed she had returned.

Wearing a sundress in some kind of filmy white fabric, her hair piled loosely on top of her head, Talitha was standing side on to him, one foot resting on her calf as if she was performing a tree pose. She had a sketchbook in one hand and a pen in the other, and her forehead was creased in concentration.

As he stepped forward, a twig cracked beneath his foot. It sounded like a pistol going off. She spun round sharply and he got a glimpse of wide brown eyes as she almost fell over.

'What are you playing at?' Recovering her balance, she glared at him.

'I could ask you the same thing.'

There was a long silence, and he got the sense that she was biting back her irritation when she said stiffly, 'I'm drawing the temple.' Glancing away, she stared across the lake. 'Is it possible to get over there?'

'It is. There's a boat. I'll show you.'

He led her to the boat in the boathouse, slotting the oars into place as she stepped in.

'What are you doing?' Her eyes widened as he dropped onto the bench opposite her and picked up the oars.

'Coming with you, obviously,' he said blandly. 'Somebody needs to row.'

Her lip curled. 'I can row a boat.'

'Not that in dress, you can't. Not if you want to keep on wearing it anyway.'

She gave him another of those haughty little stares, and then, scooping up her skirt, swung her legs over the bench so that her back was facing him.

His gaze snagged on the hollow at the hairline of her neck, sending heat skimming across his skin.

Being alone with Talitha on an island, with her in that dress, was an extraordinarily bad idea. Every instinct he had was screaming at him to turn the boat around. But instead he carried on rowing, and it was easier than he thought to lose himself in the rhythm of lifting and dipping the oars into the cool, clear water.

'Is it all right to go inside?' she asked as he tied up the boat and helped her onto the island.

He nodded. 'Be my guest.'

If the length of her hem wasn't distraction enough, she had paired the dress with those sandals that wrapped around and up the leg, and as he watched her weave between the columns he felt such a throb of desire that he had to walk away to compose himself.

Only now, having walked in opposite directions, they met head-on.

She stopped first, her eyes fixing on his face, and he saw her shoulders straighten.

More to maintain the upper hand than because he wanted to see, he held out his hand. 'May I see what you were drawing?'

After a short, appraising silence, she handed him the sketchbook.

To his knowledge, Talitha had never drawn anything during their entire relationship. Now, looking down at her sketch, he wondered why.

'I didn't know you could draw.'

Her eyebrow rose into an arch as perfect as any at Rome's Colosseum. 'I could fill a library with books about all the things you don't know about me, Dante.'

He let that go. Flipping over the pages, he saw that she had drawn all the downstairs rooms of the villa, and that the first sketch had been just that—a sketch. The others were finished and they were good. More than good. They were mesmerising. The brushstrokes seemed almost to float on top of the paper, so that rather than obscuring the shape and form underneath they brought them to life.

'So you fill in the colour later?'

She nodded. 'It helps. I don't have a very good visual memory.' Her eyes darted to his face: a tiny, tentative upward flick, so quick he thought he'd imagined it, and then a flush of colour crept upwards over her cheekbones.

'But you take photos?'

Another nod. 'Yes, because nothing can beat the precision of a photograph. But this isn't about accuracy—it's about preserving the mood of an interior, even if there is a photographic record.'

'And why do you need to preserve the mood?'

'Because, for me, mood is as important as scale or light. If you get it right the art breathes; you give it life.'

Her voice had changed. There was a seriousness to it now. He realised with shock that he had misread her again. Curating was more than a job to her. She cared.

He stared down at her, a pulse of excitement beating down his spine. 'May I keep these?'

She blinked. 'I don't usually— I mean, they're just something I do for myself.'

'Is that a no?'

She hesitated. 'Maybe I could do you copies,' she said finally.

'I'd like that.' He flipped back through the sketchbook to the Temple of Diana. 'What's this?'

At the centre of the temple she had drawn an outline, the cross-hatched body incomplete, yet recognisably female.

'It's Diana. It's a futuristic interpretation of a Romanesque statue by an Italian artist called Stefano Riva.'

'I like it. What's it made of?'

'Stainless steel.'

He stared down at the figure, then back to the bare plinth where the original Diana had stood. It was perfect.

'Can we get it?'

'I think so. He's an emerging artist, so prices should be well within the budget.' She gave him a small uncertain smile. 'It's actually coming up for auction on Thursday, at Sotheby's in Milan.'

Milan.

His body tensed and he stared down at her, looking for a flicker of emotion in her beautiful face. But he saw nothing, and he felt his jaw set tight. That she could so easily consider a return to the city where their relationship had imploded was more proof of how little it—*he*—had meant to her.

She might be happy to return, but he wasn't. And as for an auction…

He felt his stomach clench. After all these years it was unlikely that anyone would connect crypto-currency billionaire Dante King with the Dante Cannavaro who had grown up in a Naples slum, but here in Italy, even more so than in the US, he avoided public appearances.

He handed back the sketchbook. 'I don't have time to go to an auction.'

'I wasn't expecting *you* to go.'

The startled expression on her face made his jaw tighten and he felt the ground ripple beneath his feet. Back in England, his plan had been simple. He'd wanted to bring Talitha to heel, curtail her as he'd failed to do in Milan. So why, then, did it feel as if she was still out of reach?

He knew why. She might be doing it under the guise

of being very efficient, very professional, but she was trying to avoid him. Suddenly he was fighting to get on top of his anger.

'My apologies,' he said coolly. 'I expressed myself badly. What I meant to say was *you* don't have time to go.'

Talitha stared at him mutely. Her heart was pounding so hard that it was making her body shake.

She was such an idiot. Last night, watching him prowl the garden in the darkness, she had actually been worried about him. Despite everything that had happened, everything he had done, she'd let herself care.

But she was done caring for this infuriating, judgemental man. He had hurt her on so many levels and she wouldn't be hurt by him anymore. She certainly wasn't going to let herself slide back down into that place she'd been three years ago.

'This was your idea, Dante,' she hissed. 'You insisted that I come out here. Yet all you want to do is bring up the past—and we could have done that in London. I'm trying to make this work, but I'm starting to think you're not really committed to building a collection at all.'

She was getting out of breath, but she couldn't stop herself. Anger was swelling inside her, filling her up so that suddenly she was no longer a person but an outlet for her fury.

'But I suppose I shouldn't be surprised. You always had commitment issues. Why should this be any different?'

His eyes locked on to hers. 'That's not how I re-member it.'

'Then you must have a very selective memory. Or have you forgotten what happened in Milan?'

He took a step towards her, and she could see the anger smouldering in his eyes.

'Oh, no. I remember everything that happened in Milan. I remember saying goodbye to you, and texting you from the airport. I remember walking back into the apartment three weeks later and you being gone. I remember there being no note.'

'There was nothing to say,' she snapped. 'You said it all by going to America *without me*. Going home to your family *without me*. You didn't want me involved.'

He shook his head. 'Not this again.'

'Yes, "this again",' she snapped.

'Why would you go with me, Talitha?'

All of a sudden she felt as if they were back in Milan. He was looking at her with just the same mix of frustration and caution. She could almost feel him closing himself off from her.

'We'd been dating for four months.'

'We weren't *dating*, Dante. We were engaged.' Her heart was hard and heavy in her chest. 'And your mother was in hospital.'

'It was cataract surgery. She didn't even have an anaesthetic. There was no need to drag you halfway around the world.'

She gave a brittle laugh. 'You wouldn't have been dragging me. I wanted to go with you.' She had wanted to be there for him. Only of course that had been the last thing he'd wanted.

'So you said at the time.' The ice in his voice burned her skin. 'And yet strangely, twenty-one days later, you left me. So perhaps we should be talking about your commitment issues, not mine.'

The memory of those weeks—her frantic phone calls, the crushing uncertainty and confusion—made her shake inside. 'Don't you dare make this about me. You didn't call me or answer my calls for days.'

'I only waited because—'

She interrupted. 'Because you were too busy furthering your career.'

Meeting people she had introduced him to.

A muscle flickered in his jaw. 'I didn't plan that, but I wasn't going to turn down the opportunity.'

'And you can't see why I might have had a problem with that.'

'A problem! You upped and left me.' The frustration in his voice turned Dante's words into a rasp, like a blade scraping across a stone.

'No, I didn't. I sat around like a mug and waited.'

Even though she'd known that he didn't care for her the way she cared for him, she had loved him so much she would have waited until the end of time.

'Only then I bumped into Nick Coates, and he told me he'd met up with you in New York. *At the office.*'

Doing what mattered to him the most.

'I met up with him for you—for us.'

Pain cut through her anger. 'There was no "us", Dante. There was only ever you.'

His face hardened. 'So in Milan, when we walked around the city until dawn the night we first met, was that about me or was it about us? When I brought you breakfast in bed and we ended up staying there all day—was that about us?'

Yes, she had thought so, at the time, and even now she wanted it to have been...

She felt suddenly exhausted. What was the point of any of this? Dante had made up his mind about what had happened a long time ago, and no amount of analysing the past was going to change his opinion of her.

'It doesn't matter anyway,' she said dully. 'I don't even know why we're talking about it. There's no going back.'

The journey over to the island had been tense but, if anything, the return trip was even more strained. She sat facing away from him again, it was easier that way, but she could still feel his gaze drilling into her back.

She frowned. He had stopped rowing. 'What is it?' Turning, she felt her muscles tense. His eyes were locked on her face.

'You should have waited for me,' he said.

'I told you. I did.'

'Why didn't you wait longer?'

Pain seared through her. She had been exhausted, and desperate not to lose him, but scared of how easy he'd found it to cut her out of his life. Just like her parents had done—like they still did.

Tears pricked her eyes and, hating how he still had the power to anger her and hurt her like no one else, she answered without thinking. 'Because when people go, they don't come back. I didn't need to waste any more of my life waiting around for someone who could so easily forget me.'

She had done enough of meeting her parents halfway, only to realise all the effort was on her side and not theirs.

His gaze was intent. 'What people?'

She felt panic slither down her spine. She didn't need his judgement. Or, worse, his pity. 'It doesn't matter,' she said quickly.

Her eyes darted past him to the bank of the lake, and for one mad moment she actually considered jumping in and swimming back. But something in his face told her that she would be wasting her time, and that he would be relentless in his pursuit of an answer.

Taking a breath, she said quickly, 'When I was seven, my father went off with the mother of my best friend from school.' She swallowed past the lump in her throat. 'A few months later my mother dropped me off at my grandparents for the holidays. Neither of them came back.'

A silence stretched out between them.

His face was like stone. 'That must have been painful. Do you see them now?'

She looked away, not wanting him to see the tears in her eyes that would reveal how much the revelation was costing her. 'My father, almost never. My mother, maybe once every two or three years. I don't fit in with their lives, and that's fine. I'm not a child.'

She had spent so long trying to be strong and independent, pretending to everyone that everything was fine. It was strange finally saying the words out loud. And oddly, a relief.

'And you thought I was like them?'

Her heart contracted. *Yes.* Except it wasn't that simple.

Maybe it would have been different if one of her parents had stayed. Losing one parent was unfortunate, but to lose two looked a lot like a pattern. And the only common denominator was her. She was clearly the problem, and deep down she had always been waiting for him to discover the real Talitha—the one who was not worthy of being in his life.

She just hadn't expected it to happen so quickly.

'Maybe subconsciously,' she said. 'I don't think I was rational about it.'

There was no 'think' about it. Why else, aside from a complete loss of reason, would she have proposed to him?

After witnessing the devastating erosion of her parents' marriage she had been adamant that she would never marry. Right up until the moment she'd met Dante, and then she would have done anything to keep him—including propose to him.

'Why didn't you tell me?' he asked quietly.

She stared at him, shivering inside. More importantly, why had she told him now? Why stir everything up after all this time?

'It never seemed to be the right time.' Her focus had been on the present with him, never the past.

His face stiffened and she thought he might be about to cross-examine her, unpick her motives, but instead he said quietly, 'I don't understand how someone could treat a child like that. Especially a parent. It's unforgivable.'

Glancing up, she felt her throat clench. Even in profile she could sense his discomfort. But how could someone like him understand? He came from the archetypal Italian family. One adored child. Two doting parents. And he was a son as well.

'Some people just aren't meant to be parents.'

'No, they're not. But you deserved better. A lot better. I'm sorry.'

She stared up at him in confusion. Whatever she had been expecting him to say, it wasn't that.

'I'm sorry,' he said again, and this time he reached out and laid his hand over hers.

Her heartbeat stumbled. His hand felt warm and firm, and it seemed to heal a little of the pain she had carried for so long. 'It's okay. It was a long time ago.'

'I wasn't talking about your parents. I was talking about how I behaved.'

He was staring at her so intently she felt his gaze like the touch of his hand on her face.

'I didn't mean to hurt you, Talitha—'

He broke off, glancing upwards. She felt the air shiver, registered that the surface of the lake had turned dark, and then a few, fat warm raindrops fell from the sky and it started to rain hard. Seconds later torrents of water were sheeting down, dancing off the lily pads and drenching them in seconds. Above them the bruised sky bellowed like an angry god, and she gasped as a fork of light splintered the blue.

Lifting her face, she closed her eyes, conscious of nothing but the warm water and the snatch of her breath. And then, just like that, the rain stopped. Squinting through damp lashes, she looked across the lake to see a rainbow, arcing above the meadow like an iridescent bead curtain.

But only for a moment, and then she turned back to Dante.

'I never want to hurt you,' he said quietly, and only then did she realise that their knees were touching.

She turned towards him slowly and felt all the air leave her body. He was staring at her so intently that she couldn't move out of his gaze, and she was suddenly acutely conscious of how her dress was clinging to her body, the soaked fabric revealing not only the lace of her bra and panties but the outline of her taut nipples.

Something stirred low down in her pelvis.

His clothes were wet too, his shirt sticking to his powerful body so that she could see the contours of his muscles.

Mouth dry, she lifted her chin and his eyes locked with hers. And then her pulse stalled as he reached out and smoothed a strand of damp hair behind her ear. His thumb strummed against her cheek and for a moment they just stared at one another. And then she leaned forward and kissed him.

She felt heat rush through her as his fingers slid through her hair and he drew her head back with a tug, his mouth covering hers, his lips and tongue urgent.

Her belly clenched, tightening around the ache

building there, and then he was pulling her closer, the hard muscles of his arms wrapping around her, pressing her against his chest, and the heat flared into something fierce and demanding.

CHAPTER SIX

SHAKING WITH DESIRE, she shifted against him and he lifted her onto his lap, the movement causing the boat to judder alarmingly. Neither of them cared. Nothing mattered except the touch of his hands, the jagged rush of his breath, the rasp of his stubble against her face.

He was kissing her wet neck now, and then his hands slid over her shoulders, pulling down the sleeves and the straps of her bra, exposing her breasts to the warm, damp air as the boat spun in slow, sweeping circles.

But only for a moment. And then his mouth latched onto the nipple and she felt her body come to life. She arched against him, feeling the hard press of his erection, feeling an answering wetness between her thighs that had nothing to do with the rain.

Breathing out raggedly, she pushed his shirt up from his trousers, tugging at his belt buckle, a grunt of frustration breaking from her lips as her damp fingers slipped against the zip and then finally—thank goodness—finally she freed him.

The feel of him took her breath away. He was so hot and hard. Her fingers trembled against the smooth, pulsing length of him, and then he was pushing aside the scrap of lace between her thighs, and she felt his hand move between them, unerringly finding the taut bud of her clitoris, touching her, caressing her in a way that made her breath clog.

She shuddered, pressing closer, wanting more, needing more, needing the ache inside her to be answered. Her eyelashes fluttered shut and, lifting her hips, she opened her legs, stroking the taut, swollen head of his erection back and forth against the slick heat, a little deeper each time. And then he was pushing inside her.

Someone moaned; she had no idea if it was him or her.

They were clinging to one another as if they were drowning. His hand was clamped against her back, drawing her closer, bodies moving in tandem, their edges blurring.

His pulse was filling her head. Her skin was hot. She was melting into him. Flames were dancing inside her eyelids and she was lost to everything but the heat and the urgency of her desire as she felt him grow inside her, swelling, filling her.

A streak of fire snaked through her and she reared against him, her body tightening on the inside as he thrust upwards, the friction building, hotter and hotter. She took a breath, her pulse beating out a drumroll of need, rocking her hips, chasing the fierce white heat, her pulse quickening as he thrust deeper and harder. And then she jerked against him, her body gripping his tightly, so tightly, her back flexing beneath his hands, muscles spasming in a breathless frenzy of pleasure.

He groaned her name, his body arching, his fingers tightening in her hair, his breath hot against her throat as he slammed into her, shuddering convulsively.

Body twitching, she leaned into him limply, her sweaty skin sticking to his face. His jerky breath was hot in her hair, and beneath the thundering of her heart she could just about hear the sound of insects hovering above the water.

She could have stayed there for ever with her eyes closed. The sun was warm on her back, her body felt soft and sated, and Dante's hand was deliciously heavy, draped around her waist. But she knew she should move.

And not just because someone might come along at any moment and catch them *in flagrante*.

Muscles clenching inside, she squeezed her eyes more tightly shut.

There were two ways of dealing with this situation. Two possible things that could happen next but only one which should. Obviously the thing that wasn't going to happen was the two of them tearing at each other's clothes and mating like animals in the open air again.

That left only one alternative. To tell him firmly and clearly that this was a crazy thing to have done, and the best and the only thing to do now was to move forward as if it hadn't happened.

'I didn't ask—'

Dante's voice cut through her thoughts and she felt his hand lift away from her body as she sat up straighter. With a jolt, she realised he was still fully dressed and, suddenly acutely aware of her bare breasts, and how her dress was rucked up above her thighs, she felt heat flame in her cheeks.

He probably couldn't believe his luck. Not only had he managed to take her with next to no disruption, but she had spurred him on, clutching his erection as if she had never held one before, climbing up to straddle his muscular body in her hunger.

Remembering the noises she had made, and how frantic she had been, she felt another wave of heat wash over her body and, clutching at the front of her dress to cover herself, she clambered back onto the other bench.

Leaning forward to smooth her skirt, she let her hair fall in front of her scalded face. 'Ask what?'

She heard the rasp of his zip. 'If you were protected.'

Protected! She glanced up at him, blinking. Thankfully, she was. But it had all happened so fast that truthfully it hadn't even crossed her mind.

Trying to keep her voice steady, she nodded. 'Yes, I am.'

She had thought he would be relieved but, glancing up at his face, she saw that there was tension around his mouth.

'Good,' he said at last. 'And you don't need to worry about me. I'm careful.' He hesitated, his voice stiffening. 'I suppose we should talk about this.'

If she hadn't been so shocked she might almost have laughed.

Dante was offering to talk.

When they'd been together it was what she had wanted most, but he'd always held a part of himself in check. Only now it was happening she could feel herself shying away from the prospect of discussing her blatant, febrile need.

Tearing her gaze away from his dark, perfect profile, she said quickly, 'I don't think that's necessary. I mean, it's not as if it's going to happen again.'

Dante stared at her in silence, his muscles aching with the effort it was taking not to pull her against him and prove her wrong. But that would mean revealing how badly he wanted her, and he had got close enough to embarrassing himself already today.

He'd been so eager and hard for her that he'd only just managed to hold himself back until he was inside of her. Worse, he'd been so caught up in his hunger that he'd actually forgotten about a condom.

Staring past her, to where the drenched landscape shimmered in the sunlight, he tried to persuade his famous and feared *sang-froid* to return.

The whole encounter had lasted less than five minutes, but he had felt it with the obliterating force of a thunderbolt. Just like in Milan, there had been a oneness between them, so that in those few frenzied moments it had been impossible to say where he stopped and she began.

But that was how it was with Talitha.

How it had always been with Talitha.

And he wanted her again—wanted her already, wanted more. He wanted to touch her, caress her, lick every inch of her skin, mould her body against his.

He felt his blood pound, hot and fast.

She wanted the same. So why not kiss her again? Why not go back to the villa and up to her room and strip her naked? Keep her there until he'd exhausted this hunger they had reawakened.

There was such a terrible, tempting logic to that idea that he had to clamp his hands beside his thighs to stop himself from reaching across the boat for her. But that itself proved how off-key his thinking was right now. He'd already made enough mistakes with this woman, letting passion override common sense, believing love could surmount all obstacles. He didn't need to make any more.

'Agreed. Sex with the ex has a certain *piccantezza*,' he said coolly. 'But I think that particular itch has been sufficiently scratched now.' Reaching past her, he took hold of the oars and lowered them into the water. 'We should probably be getting back.'

She nodded. 'I think so.'

She glanced away as she spoke, and her voice was smooth and chilled like vintage champagne. Something tightened inside him. He should be relieved that they were on the same page, but instead he was stung by just how quickly and easily she could dismiss their frantic coupling.

'You would never have told me, would you?' He stared at her steadily. 'About your parents.'

Her eyes narrowed. 'Would you have wanted to know?'

'Of course.'

There was a beat of silence, and then she breathed

out shakily. 'What do you mean, "of course"? You weren't exactly into sharing. You still aren't.'

He stared down at her. 'You moved into my apartment in Milan. You're staying in my home now. I'd say that makes me pretty good at sharing.'

Her arms were folded in front of her like a shield. 'I don't mean *things*, Dante. I mean feelings—all the stuff going on in your head. Like why you were pacing around your garden in the middle of the night.'

There was a long, quivering pause. 'I'd been working for hours,' he said at last. 'I needed some fresh air.'

As answers went it was perfectly plausible, but as he watched her shoulders stiffen he knew that Talitha was not convinced.

But what was he supposed to say? He could hardly tell her the real reason he had been prowling around the garden in the dark. Although three years ago he had come close—closer than at any time before or since. Besotted and reckless with love, he had been on the verge of telling her everything about his family.

His biological family.

It was the first time he had even imagined sharing the truth with anyone, and he had been so scared. That was why he had agreed to meet with Nick Coates in New York. He had wanted to have something to show Talitha—something to cancel out the ugliness of his past. Proof that although he shared their bloodline he wasn't a Cannavaro, that he was different, that he could take care of her.

That she could trust him.

Only as it turned out, he hadn't been able to trust her.

His stomach clenched and he gripped the oars, his fingers tightening around the leather handles as if to anchor himself. But of course, it wasn't as simple as that. And it didn't sit well, finding out that he had misjudged her. Or that she had imagined her only option was to run back to England.

Thinking back to what Talitha had told him about her parents made his throat tighten. He felt ashamed. No wonder she had run from him. He would have run too.

A knot was forming in his stomach. He had run—and was still running. Running from the past, and running from the fear of who he might become if the past caught up with him.

And with both of them running it was hardly surprising that they had ended up so far apart. Or that they had wrecked everything.

Not quite everything, he thought, his body tensing, thinking back to the velvet heat of her mouth on his.

His shoulders tensed as he drew back the oars. That was his fault too. The predictable result of an abstinence that had stretched on far too long. He should have found some other woman to satisfy his physical needs, but that was easier than it sounded. Talitha might have walked out of his life in Milan, but whenever he had thought about sex, or considered seeing someone else, it had been her face that swam inside his head, her soft, pouting mouth begging him for release.

His breath hitched, his groin hardening with a surge of testosterone, and as he shifted against the hard wooden bench, he swore silently. How was that even possible?

But he knew from experience that it wasn't just possible with Talitha—it was inevitable. One touch was never enough.

Cursing himself silently for his weakness, he concentrated the throb of his libido on the task in hand, rowing back across the lake with smooth, efficient strokes, slicing through the lily pads with an almost savage pleasure. Inside the boathouse, he climbed out swiftly and held out his hand. She took it, then hesitated, her eyes darting back to the boat.

'My sketchbook—' She reached down and fumbled beneath the thwart, then stood up slowly, biting her lip.

Water dripped from the pages; the beautiful crisp sketches looked more like Florentine marbled paper.

He stared down at it, felt something wrenching inside him, and without thinking he reached out and touched her hand.

'Don't.' She jerked her arm away.

'Talitha...'

'Just leave me alone, Dante.' He reached for her again but she swerved past him, ducking out of the boathouse, and he watched the pale soles of her shoes as she ran across the meadow and disappeared from view.

Reaching the villa, hot and out of breath, Talitha felt her legs stiffen and slow. She had hoped to slip inside unnoticed, but the housekeeper was waiting anxiously on the terrace, a folded umbrella tucked under her arm.

'Hi Angelica.' Smoothing her damp dress, she pinned a smile on her face.

'Signorina Hamilton... Thank goodness.' The housekeeper's eyes widened as they took in Talitha's dishevelled appearance. 'But you got caught in the rain.'

'It's fine, really. I'm practically dry now,' Talitha lied, feeling suddenly self-conscious about her clothing. Had she fastened everything up? Or was something on show that shouldn't be?

Angelica tutted. 'I should have sent Mauro to look for you with the buggy.'

Talitha felt her cheeks burn. Even the idea of Mauro witnessing what had happened on the boat made her stomach churn. The last thing she needed was that moment of weakness existing independently of her and Dante.

As if Angelica could read her thoughts, she glanced past her. 'Did Mr King find you?'

She felt her heartbeat trip over itself.

Yes, he had found her.

Or, to be more accurate, they had found each other. And, much as she didn't want to admit it, even to herself, on some subconscious level at least she knew that the two of them had conspired to make that happen.

Dante could have asked Arielle to curate his collection.

He could have put her up in a hotel in Siena, not in his home.

And she could have insisted on staying in a hotel. Or gone to the island another time, on her own.

Instead, she had kissed him, and then she'd had sex with him.

'He did. He had something to do,' she said vaguely. Her jaw was aching now with the effort of smiling. 'I think I might go and tidy up. Could you tell Mr King that I'll catch up with him later?'

Still smiling, she escaped up the stairs. Closing the door behind her, she let her smile fade and sank shakily to the floor.

The sodden sketchbook slipped from her fingers. She couldn't quite believe what she had done—what *they* had done. After that kiss in the Hanover she had known that Dante was playing with her.

Only they hadn't been playing in the boat.

She pressed her knees together, felt the muscles of her legs tightening around the stickiness and the ache between her thighs.

It had been real.

Hot and primal and irresistible.

Her heart thumped against her ribs as she pictured the dark fire in his eyes as he thrust inside her. Sex hadn't been part of the plan, but that blazing hunger had transformed him into the man she had fallen in love with.

So of course she'd had sex with him.

Only it shouldn't have happened.

Just as she shouldn't have told him about her parents.

A breeze from the balcony drifted across her face and she put her hand to a cheek that now burned for a different reason.

Three years ago he had left her behind in Italy to go and see his family in the States. And whatever he said now, about their not knowing each other for very long, it had been glaringly obvious that he didn't want to share his life with her. Nothing had changed. Look at how he'd fobbed her off when she'd asked why he'd been walking in the garden.

Remembering how she had watched him from the window, she felt her skin tighten. She had been idiotic enough to feel sorry for him, but no more. Dante had broken her heart and if that wasn't enough he had blackmailed her into coming out here.

And yet you just had sex with him as if none of that mattered, said an accusing little voice inside her head.

She hugged her knees to her chest.

On every possible level it was wrong, and yet she still couldn't imagine a timeline where it wouldn't have happened.

Staring blindly across the room, in her head she saw the moment when he had slipped her dress from her shoulders, saw his hands moving feverishly over her hot, bare skin, and she knew that if she closed her eyes she would almost feel Dante's mouth on her breast.

She licked her lips, feeling the softness and the soreness. Hadn't she learned anything? Surely she knew better than to get too close to the flame.

Situations changed: people didn't. Everybody was on a fixed path. The good ones, like her grandparents, were always there for you, always trustworthy and reliable. The rest might converge briefly with you on your journey, but believing you were their destination and not just a stop enroute was a mug's game.

Her parents had taught her that lesson again and again. Only it was difficult not to keep hoping that the next time would be different.

Glancing down, she caught sight of a red mark on her collarbone, where Dante's stubble had rasped against her skin, and a ripple of desire pulsed across her skin.

It was even more difficult when there was a lingering echo of attraction.

But she couldn't ignore the truth. Not this time.

When it came to the crunch, when he'd had the choice to have her by his side, he hadn't wanted or needed her. He'd been too busy building his empire.

She took a quick, hot shower, turning the jets of water on full, washing away every trace of Dante from her body, wishing she could do the same with her mind.

Smoothing her hair into a low ponytail, she picked out a pale green dress with bell sleeves and a pair of nude heels for added height. After days of wearing sandals they felt a little on the tight side. But she didn't care. In fact, it was probably a good thing. Pain was just what she needed to clear her head.

And she needed a clear head to set up a telephone bid for the Riva statue.

A hollow ache spread beneath her ribs. She was so excited about the statue that she had actually been prepared to go to Milan—back to the city where she had let passion override common sense, and paid the price.

Only even now there was a certain twisted appeal

to the idea. She could see how returning alone might offer a kind of closure. But his blunt refusal to let her go had simply confirmed that this entire trip was just an opportunity for Dante to punish her.

As if he hadn't already punished her enough.

She was just checking the reserve price in the catalogue when her laptop screen abruptly turned black. Glancing down at the battery icon, she swore softly. How could she have let that happen? And then she swore again, this time more loudly, as she realised that she had left her charger in the drawing room.

Gritting her teeth, she stalked across the room and wrenched open the door.

'What the—?'

Her heart thumping wildly in her ears, she rocked back on her heels with shock.

Dante was standing in front of her door, his arm frozen in the act of knocking.

A prickling heat darted across her skin. Unlike her, he hadn't bothered changing his clothes, and his slightly crumpled appearance instantly conjured up an image of the two of them coupling frantically in the boat.

'Sorry, I didn't mean to startle you,' he said.

There was nothing in his voice—no stress, no hint of intimacy—to suggest that anything had even happened. Instead, he sounded perfectly composed. She clenched her hands by her sides, no longer squirming but indignant. Clearly he had no regrets or concerns about what they had done.

'I wanted to give you this.'

He was holding a bunch of folders and, reaching between them, he extricated a box.

'What is it?'

'It's a sketchbook. To replace the one that got ruined in the rain. I know you need it to work.'

She stared at him, shaking inside with the force of her indignation and hurt. Unbelievably, and yet entirely predictably, he had already moved on from their sexual encounter to what mattered to him most.

Work.

Part of her wanted to ask how he could do that. But she wasn't going to reveal the depth of her hurt or let him think that it had meant more to her than it had to him.

'You didn't have to do that. I have a spare one.'

Could she sound any more ungrateful?

Very slowly, he lifted his gaze to meet hers. 'I know I didn't have to.' There was a dangerous edge to his voice, like sharpened steel sheathed in silk. 'I wanted to.'

And what Dante wanted, he got, she thought, swallowing past the ache in her throat. And he wanted copies of the sketches she'd made.

Ignoring his outstretched hand, she folded her arms in front of her body. 'Why? So you can throw it back in my face afterwards? Chalk it up as another example of my bad character? Well, you didn't need to bother. I already know what you think of me.'

Her eyes snagged on the bare skin of her finger, where she had briefly worn his engagement ring.

How little he thought of her. How easily he'd been able to forget her.

It was going to rain again. The air felt thick, and behind her the bedroom was growing darker. She felt panic grab her by the throat. She felt exposed, trapped by her own stupidity and a feeling of there being no way out.

'I thought you were upset. I just wanted to do the right thing.'

There was a note she didn't recognise in his voice and she looked up at him in confusion, noticing the flattened mouth and the tension in his shoulders. But she was done with caring about what was going on inside Dante's head. He'd cured her of that.

'You? Do the right thing?' Her mouth twisted. Right or wrong was irrelevant. He didn't do anything unless it suited him. 'I don't think that's genetically possible, Dante.'

His eyes darkened like the surface of the lake when the clouds had moved in front of the sun. He stared at her in silence for a few pulsing seconds, and then he put the box down on the table with a gentleness that made something pinch inside her.

'I have no use for a sketchbook. So if you don't want it then perhaps you can give it to someone else. I'll leave you to get on with your work.'

He turned and walked away before she could reply and she stared after him, a hard, heavy lump filling her throat. Aside from the more glamorous setting, and a few changes to the dialogue, it was essentially a replay of how he'd left her in Milan.

In other words, a masterclass in equivocation.

Fizzing with frustration, Talitha stalked back into her bedroom and slammed the door.

She was so done with his arrogance, and his assumption that everything should be done his way, and by how he was so ready to judge her but so reluctant to face his own faults.

And yet there was something about him that tunnelled deep beneath her anger. Something that made her heart squeeze painfully tight, so that even though she knew she was in the right, and he was in the wrong, she felt bereft.

She stopped in the middle of the room.

He had destroyed their love. Why, then, did he still have the power to make her care? It didn't make any sense. But then nothing about her response to this man was logical.

She snatched up the box with hands that trembled slightly. She slid off the lid and, pushing aside the cappuccino-coloured tissue paper, lifted out the sketchbook. Pulse dancing, she walked a few paces and sank onto the bed. Bound in supple leather, it was the most beautiful sketchbook she had ever seen.

It would be stupid to read anything into it. He probably hadn't even seen it. Just asked Angelica to find a replacement. She ran her fingers lightly over the pale green silk endpapers and then glanced down at her dress. Except *eau-de-nil* was her favourite colour.

A coincidence, then?

She bit her lip. Why did everything have to be so complicated with him? Just when she was happy hating him, despising him for being so cold-blooded and remote, he did this.

He was so confusing. He made her confused.

She glanced down at the sketchbook. But, whatever Dante's motives, this was still a gift. Remembering her graceless remark when he'd held out the box, she felt a sharp nip of shame.

Her grandfather would be appalled. As a child, she had been required to write thank-you cards promptly after every birthday and Christmas, and she knew that, for Edward, thanking someone for gifts, hospitality, favours, was not optional, but an absolute necessity.

She had been so wrapped up in this emotional tug of war with Dante she had lost sight of what it meant to be Edward St Croix Hamilton's granddaughter. But he was the reason she was here, and she wasn't going to let him down.

It took her over an hour to redo the sketch of the drawing room, but she was more than satisfied with the result. The paper in the sketchbook was of such good quality that it gave a wonderful depth to the gouache.

She felt calmer now. More in control. *More herself.*

Ready to face Dante.

Or so she thought. But as she rounded the corner to go downstairs her footsteps faltered. Dante was walking out of his bedroom, a phone clamped against his ear.

He said something in Italian she didn't understand and hung up.

'I didn't mean to interrupt you,' she said quickly.

'It wasn't important. Do you want me for something?'

Her pulse twitched, and she felt heat ripple across her skin as her brain offered up several all equally X-rated answers to that question.

She hesitated. 'Actually, yes. I wanted you to know that I've just finished redoing the painting of the drawing room.'

'You still think that's why I gave you the sketchbook?'

His voice was cool and even, but his eyes had narrowed fractionally, and she felt her earlier certainty bleed away. Why had she thought this would be simple?

'Yes… No… I don't know. But that's the point,' she said quickly. 'It doesn't matter.'

There was a silence. Then, 'So what are you saying?'

What was she saying? Head spinning, she groped for the words. 'Thank you. I wanted to say thank you. That's all.'

'Wait.'

The tension in his voice stopped her as she turned away.

'You wanted to thank me?'

His hesitancy caught a nerve. But why did she care so much what he thought of her? 'You're not the only one who wants to do the right thing,' she said quickly.

'Talitha…'

Her body quivered with the effort of facing him. 'I'm not looking for a fight, Dante.'

A muscle flickered in his jaw. 'I'm not either.'

She gave a shaky laugh that almost became a sob. 'And yet somehow we always end up fighting.'

There was another silence.

'Not always,' he said quietly.

Her gaze skidded towards his face and she shook her head. She had to think about him without any reference to the past or the pull of their hunger.

'We can't… I can't—' She shook her head again as he took a step towards her.

'Would it help if I told you that I want you so badly I can't think straight?'

The bluntness of his words made her breath catch fire. 'And I want you,' she admitted.

She knew she was giving away too much, letting him know the power he wielded, but somehow it seemed important to be honest with him.

'Only wanting isn't enough. I know people say it is, and it was for me in the boat. But that was different. It wasn't planned.'

It had been pure animal desire—a force of nature. Wild and mindless and excusable. But consciously choosing to have sex with a man who didn't like her, much less love her, was just too cold-blooded.

His eyes didn't leave hers. 'So what are you suggesting? That we just ignore it? Walk away?'

Something in his voice made her chest ache so that she could hardly breathe. 'You want it to be just sex. But it isn't. It can't be because of what happened before. And in case you've forgotten that didn't work for either of us then, and nothing's changed.'

'Everything's changed. We're different people now.'

Had it? Were they?

'Okay, then, if you're different tell me something true about you,' she challenged. 'Something I don't know.'

He stared at her in silence, his eyes distant, his expression shuttered, and she felt a sick lurch in her stomach. With all her heart she wished that she could take it all back, return to her bedroom, to England. She could no longer even remember why she was doing this.

'I came after you,' he said quietly. 'After I got back to Milan, I came to London to find you.'

CHAPTER SEVEN

TALITHA STARED AT DANTE in stunned silence.

A part of her wanted to accuse him of lying, but she knew from the tension radiating from his body that he was telling the truth.

'When…? How—?'

'About a month after you left. I made up some story and got your address from Nick, and then I flew to London and went to the townhouse.' He stared past her as if was looking back in time. 'I bought you roses. Only when I knocked on the door a man answered.'

She felt her heart stall. *Ned.* Dante had met Ned.

'He thought I was delivering flowers, and when I said that they were for you he said that it was okay to leave them with him because he was your fiancé.'

Her breath was clogging her throat. There had been flowers, lots of flowers, before she'd had a chance to speak to Ned. She could remember being appalled that she had let it get so far.

His mouth twisted. 'I didn't correct him. There didn't seem much point.'

She felt dizzy, as if an earthquake had shaken the

landscape and everything she'd thought she knew—
everything that had seemed so solid and unchange-
able—now looked completely different.

'I didn't know,' she said hoarsely.

A band was tightening around her ribs. She felt as
if she'd had a terrible dream and was trapped in it.

What had they done? What had *she* done?

'I know.' He spoke so quietly that his words were
nearly drowned out by the sound of the thundering rain.

There was a silence.

'I know you've spent the morning telling yourself
what happened on the lake was a mistake, because I
have too,' he said at last. 'Only I can't stop thinking
about you. You're always there in my head. When I
wake you're lying there beside me. I can't get undressed
at night without undressing you too.' He cleared his
throat. 'I'll walk away if that's what you want. But I
don't think either of us will ever be free until we let
this…' his eyes captured hers, holding her, letting her
know what he wanted '…run its course.'

Her heartbeat was filling her head.

Dante had come after her.

She had been wrong about that, just as he had been
wrong about her being engaged to Ned. It was exactly
like one of those Shakespearean plays, with confusing titles and complicated plots about mistaken identity, where everyone ended up with the right person
in the end.

*Except she and Dante were neither with nor right
for each other.*

From somewhere above came a low, warning rumble.

She shook her head. 'We can't go back. It's too late. What we had…it's gone.'

'I'm not talking about going back.'

He took a step closer, the intensity in his eyes rooting her to the spot. Now there was only a hair-fine gap between them.

'The past has no bearing on this. It'll be like we never met. We'll just be two strangers hooking up in a bar.'

His words caught her off guard.

Two strangers in a bar.

That was when they had worked. When it had been just a blur of sex and food and sleep and sex. When it had been a no-strings holiday affair in the sun. Before fear had entered the relationship.

Her fear. That he would leave her. That history would repeat itself.

But there was nothing to fear in what Dante was suggesting now. The past had been erased and the future too, and this time she knew what she was getting into. This was passion, not love, and instead of feeling scared of the uncertainties she felt powerful, and for the first time in their relationship his equal.

There was a tension in the air, cocooning them, pushing them together, and a tingling quiver of anticipation ran through her as he held out his hand.

'Hi, my name is Dante.'

She was shaking inside. It felt as if her life was on a pivot. Except this wasn't her life. This was make-believe.

She took his hand, playing along. 'Talitha.'

'Beautiful name…almost as beautiful as that dress you're wearing. That green is perfect on you.'

'It's called *eau-de-nil*. Water of the Nile.'

His gaze touched her like a caress, a shadow-smile pulling at his mouth. 'You're very precise about colour.'

She shrugged. 'I curate art. Colour matters to me.'

'Really? That's such a coincidence. I need a curator.'

As he spoke he took a step closer, and she felt a pulse start to beat between her thighs.

'Wait—how does this work?' She didn't recognise her own voice. 'I mean, how far are we going to go?'

She couldn't meet his eyes for fear she might be imagining it all, but then he raised his hand to her chin, tilting her face up, and she saw only certainty and a need as legible as her own.

His eyes rested on her face, the grey irises boring into her. 'All the way,' he said softly and, leaning forward, he slid his arm around her waist and covered her mouth with his.

He felt his blood turn to air.

Talitha's lips were cool and soft and, maybe because they were playing at being strangers, he was strangely reminded of the first time they'd kissed. There was the same sense of almost shock, of knowing that this was different, that it was more than just a kiss.

It was an acknowledgement of something intangible but undeniable. A communion of need.

Hunger shivered inside him and he moved his mouth across hers with deliberate slowness, taking his time. His hands slid over her ribs, moving up to her breasts.

His fingers circled the nipples and the sudden quickening of her breath made all the blood in his body surge to his groin.

She swayed against him and he felt the slide of her thigh between his legs, and then her hands moved under his shirt as they had earlier, pulling him closer and they waltzed backwards into his bedroom, like the last dancers on the floor at the end of the night.

Heart pounding, body aching, he pushed the door shut. Outside, the sky was a smouldering grey, like a fire that at any moment might catch alight, and the air was thick with moisture. In the gloom of the room, her eyes were a shade darker than normal, her skin gleaming like Carrara marble.

'Talitha…' he murmured, his voice splitting in a kind of groan. *'Sei molto bella.'*

She reached out and touched his face, her fingers feathering over the line of his jaw. 'You have a beautiful face.'

'It's just bones.'

Turning his cheek, he kissed her hand, heat flaring across his skin as her eyelashes fluttered. He stepped closer, his fingers sliding through her hair, lifting it from her neck, his mouth slipping over the doe-soft skin of her throat to the pulse beating feverishly beneath her ear.

'Undress me…'

Her words, spoken breathlessly, made his body harden so fast he thought he might black out and, reaching out dazedly, as if in a dream, he unbuttoned the front of her dress and he let it slide from her shoulders, slipping to the floor and pooling at her feet.

She was wearing no bra and he stared at her nipples, watching the tips harden in time with the jerky beat of his heart. He saw that her hands were trembling slightly. His own hands shook too, as he drew her cream-coloured panties over her hips and down her thighs to join her dress.

Heart thudding, he stared at her in silence, heat swarming over his skin.

'Now you,' she said hoarsely.

Kicking off his shoes, he yanked his shirt over his head. Then he unzipped his trousers, grimacing as he pulled them down past the erection bulking against his boxer shorts.

Their eyes met, and then he picked up her naked body and carried her over to the huge bed.

It was different from the last time. That, as Talitha said, had been unplanned. Hunger had slammed into him with a force that had knocked all thought, all memories of the past and doubts about the present, from his mind. Everything about it had been urgent, intoxicating, acute—rising up from a place where it had been dormant so long it might reasonably have been assumed that it had lost its vigour, its potency.

But it had been like a spark flaring in his blood. They had crashed together like storm clouds, their hands clumsy as they'd tried to get past the barrier of their clothes and skin. They had kissed as if they were dying of thirst, held each other as if there would be no tomorrow, her soft body moulding to his hard muscles.

But this time he took his time, sliding down her body, feeling her shiver and shift beneath him as his fingers caressed her breasts, her stomach, and then the triangle of tiny honey-coloured curls.

He lowered his mouth, tracing a line with the tip of his tongue down to part her legs. *'Amo il tuo sapore,'* he murmured.

She moaned, her fingers tightening in his hair as he pressed the flat of his tongue against the quivering, tight bud of her clitoris. His hands gripped her thighs as she started to writhe beneath him. He could hear her ragged breathing, feel the shudders racing across her skin, and then she tensed against his tongue, her body arching upwards.

Her hands fluttered against his shoulders and he pulled her down the bed, stretching her out beneath him, grunting as her fingers reached for him. He grabbed her wrist. He was so close now. One wrong move and he would lose what little control he had left.

Heart thundering, he lifted her hips slightly and pushed the blunt head of his erection inside her, the breath twisting in his throat as she locked her legs around his waist. Bracing his elbows at the shoulders, he started to move, slowly at first, then faster, losing himself in the liquid rhythm of their bodies until their skin was slick with sweat.

The blood was pulsing through his body like an express train. Placing his hand palm down on the mattress, he lifted her up, pressing her body against his in a seamless intersection of flesh and sweat. And then he heard her gasp his name, and the hot whisper of her breath tipped him over the edge and he thrust upwards, spilling into her with a groan of ecstasy.

He let his head fall forward against the hot, damp skin of her throat and then, breathing unsteadily, lifted his weight and rolled over, taking her with him, just as he'd used to do. He wasn't ready to open his eyes yet. Instead he lay still, lost in the steady pounding of the rain and the feel of her soft body curled around his.

Later—he wasn't sure when—she stirred against him and he realised he was still inside her. Still holding her close, he eased himself out. Her hand flexed against his stomach and he glanced down at her naked body, his eyes tracking along the curve of her hip.

His breath caught in his throat. This wasn't part of the plan, and yet now that it had happened he felt calmer than he had for days. It wasn't just the sex— although 'sex' felt like too mundane a word for something that had tilted his entire world on its side—it was the certainty. That was what had dogged him for so long. The sense that everything had been left hanging, unspoken, unresolved—just as if they'd both got up one morning and walked out of the apartment, leaving their clothes behind and the door wide open.

This arrangement would finally close that door.

Talitha shifted in her sleep and he glanced down at her, his eyes snagging on the dark smudges beneath her sooty lashes. Even against the crisp white pillows she looked pale, and he felt his stomach clench.

One thing was certain: he had lost all interest in punishing her. She had already suffered enough. Remembering the strain in her voice as she'd told him about her parents, he felt his skin tighten with shame. It hadn't been intentional, but he had hurt her in Milan. Pushing her away because of his own fears, never once thinking that she might be acting in self-preservation.

His mouth twisted.

Knowing what it would cost him to tell Talitha about his past, he could only imagine what it must have taken for her to reveal the truth to him—and yet even after she had bared her soul he hadn't been man enough to admit the part he'd played other than to say that she deserved better. What she really deserved was the truth.

Outside, the rain had stopped again, and he stared across the room, watching the day gain in beauty with every passing second.

He hadn't set out to lie to her. In the beginning, he had been swept off his feet in a rush of passion.

Then, when he'd realised who she was, it had been easy to persuade himself that not telling her about his birth family was no big deal. That there was a major difference between not revealing something and actually concealing it.

Then two things had happened. Talitha had proposed, and on the way back to his apartment after a night out someone had grabbed her handbag.

He felt the muscles in his arm bunch. He had chased after him, cornering the man in a side street, the blood roaring around his body. As he'd wrestled the bag free the thief had swung wildly, catching him on his mouth, and he'd hit him unthinkingly, his fists acting outside of his will.

Even now he could remember the white-hot fury that

had engulfed him. The urge to keep hitting and hurting had been like a jackhammer pounding through his body, but somehow he'd found the willpower to push the man away, holding back his rage until he was out of sight. And then he'd punched the wall until the pain in his hand had blotted out the pain in his head.

Afterwards, with the sound of bone on brick still ringing in his ears, he had been appalled—not just by the suddenness with which he had lost control, but by Talitha's distress when he'd returned with her bag and she'd seen his bloodied knuckles and cut lip.

Back at the apartment, he had looked in the bathroom mirror and seen a stranger staring back at him. Except the stranger had had a name: *Cannavaro*.

He had been repulsed, and terrified, and when his father had called the next day, to remind him about his mother's operation, he had instantly decided to go home, to get far away from Talitha. It had been the only option.

But for Talitha to understand that he'd known he would have to explain why—and that wasn't going to happen.

Only he didn't like knowing that he had made her feel as worthless as her parents...

'What are you thinking?'

Talitha's voice, drowsy with sleep, snapped his thoughts in two and, gazing down, he blanked his mind.

'I was—' he began.

But then, sitting up slightly, she pressed her fingers against his lips. 'Actually, don't answer that. I don't need to know, do I?' she whispered. And, reaching out, she looped her arm around his neck.

He felt his body throb with excitement as she pulled him closer.

It was nearly lunchtime when they finally managed to prise their bodies apart and pull on their clothes. Having done some remedial work with lipstick and eyeliner, Talitha joined Dante outside on the terrace for lunch.

'Here, let me.'

He pushed in her chair, his fingers brushing against her shoulders, and she felt a wave of anticipation ripple inside her.

Lunch was delicious, but she barely registered the food. She was too busy retracing the steps that had brought her to this moment with Dante.

Picking up her wine glass, she stared across the terrace. She felt as if her brain had split into two halves. One accepting, revelling in what it had felt like to feel the flex of his back beneath her hands and his quickening breath against her throat as he'd thrust hard and fast inside her. The other struggling to believe that she was giving herself to Dante again.

But all she was really doing was treating like with like, she thought defensively. Triggering her body's natural defences by administering a small, controlled dose of what was making her ill.

In other words, she was immunising herself against Dante.

And right now it felt good.

It felt better than good.

It felt as if she'd been let out of a cage.

The next two days and nights passed as if she were in a dream. Not once did she allow herself to think beyond the moment.

Not that thinking was her priority.

Now that the tension between them had an outlet, it was as if a dam had broken. Her hunger for him gnawed at her constantly. Whenever he was near she found herself looking at him. If he was within touching distance she couldn't not touch him.

One time, when she had gone upstairs to double-check the exact colour of one the bedroom walls, he had come to find her. She had pulled him through the door, undone his trousers, and he had lifted her skirt over her waist and pushed into her, standing up, both of them shaking like teenagers.

Except she wasn't a teenager. She was an adult with responsibilities—including, first and foremost, her grandfather. And, although she knew he was safe and being cared for, she couldn't help feeling guilty that she was wantonly spinning out these hours of pleasure with Dante rather than rushing back to England.

'What time did you say the auction was today?' he asked.

They were eating lunch on the terrace. Or rather she was eating. Dante had barely touched his food.

'Three o'clock.'

Turning her gaze towards him, she felt her heart spin like the boat on the lake. His grey eyes were staring at her steadily and the dark silky hair falling carelessly across his forehead only accentuated the sculptural perfection of his features.

Her heart skipped a beat. She had fallen in love with that face—but this wasn't about love. It was about sex and satisfaction and working him out of her system.

She gave him a small half-smile. 'Don't worry. I've set up a telephone bid.'

There was a beat of silence, and then he said quietly, 'Then you'd better cancel it.'

Her smile froze to her lips. 'I don't understand. I thought you liked the sculpture?'

'I do.' Pushing back his chair, Dante stood up and held out his hand. 'Which is why I want to be there in person.' His eyes locked with hers. 'With you. If you'll come with me?'

She stared at him, warmth tingling though her body at his words—or rather his phrasing of them. It was an invitation, not an order.

Standing up shakily, she took his hand. 'I'd like that very much…but haven't we left it too late?'

'By car, yes.'

His fingers tightened around hers, and as she watched his mouth curve up into a smile, suddenly the sun was not the brightest star in the universe.

'But we're not going by car. We're going by helicopter.'

The flight took exactly eighty minutes, and it was the perfect way to see the Tuscan countryside, Talitha decided, as they flew over cypress-lined roads, rolling green hills and golden fields dotted with sunflowers and medieval hilltop villages.

A limousine met them at a private airfield, and in no time at all they were heading through the city centre of Milan, past the upmarket boutiques in the Via Montenapoleone.

There was already a crowd outside the auction house, and as the limo slowed Talitha felt her pulse skip. Despite being a curator, she didn't actually go to that many auctions. Most of her clients opted to buy and sell privately, and there was some sense in that. But there was nothing like the rush of walking into a crowded saleroom.

'You're excited,' he said softly.

She felt her face grow warm. 'I am,' she admitted. 'I know we're not in Rome, and this isn't the Colosseum, but auctions are a lot like a gladiatorial contest. But with paddles instead of maces.'

'And an auctioneer for an emperor?' he suggested.

She smiled. 'Exactly.'

He held her gaze. 'So, how do we do this?'

We. Feeling a disproportionate throb of pleasure at Dante's use of the word, she glanced over at him. She still couldn't quite believe that they were here. He had seemed so adamant before, and she knew he was fanatical about his privacy. What could have changed his mind?

'You keep your head down and I keep my head up. Trust me. We'll get your Diana.'

She had expected him to keep his distance, but as they joined the throng of people making their way into the auction rooms she felt his hand clasp hers. Maybe he wanted to share the drama of the moment. There was something almost operatic and Baroquely brutal about the assembled collectors and speculators, circling their prey beneath the glittering chandeliers.

'Sold at two hundred and twenty-five thousand dollars!'

She glanced up, breathing in sharply as the auctioneer banged down his gavel with a flourish. Slipping between the rows of seats, she picked up the sales brochure and sat down. Dante's hands rested casually in his lap, but she could feel his iron-hard thigh pressing against hers.

'This is it,' she whispered, watching the porters carrying the covered sculpture. She felt her pulse jerk in her throat as the cover was removed, and suddenly she was shaking inside with excitement, willing the auction to begin.

'*Signore e signori*—ladies and gentlemen—next we have Lot Nineteen, an exciting opportunity to acquire a sculpture of Diana by Stefano Riva, from his New Renaissance series. I will commence the bidding at forty-five thousand dollars.'

As she'd expected, the bidding was seamlessly smooth and dizzyingly fast. Like a conductor without a baton, the auctioneer expertly read the room, shaping the emotions of the crowd as the price rose inexorably.

'We have three hundred thousand dollars—'

Talitha raised her hand, her pulse hammering inside her head. Bidding took nerves, courage, but freed from the financial constraints that dogged her everyday life she was enjoying herself.

'Three hundred and thirty thousand dollars, ladies and gentlemen, and three-fifty against you on the phone.'

Around her there was a gasp, and some applause as the bid jumped to four hundred thousand.

Pulse accelerating, she raised her hand.

'On the floor, four hundred and twenty thousand. I have four hundred and twenty thousand. Fair warning at four hundred and twenty thousand…'

The gavel hit the wood and applause filled the sale-room.

'Sold at four hundred and twenty thousand.'

Talitha felt a surge of exhilaration. People were turning to congratulate her.

'Well done,' Dante said softly. 'And thank you.'

His hand brushed against hers, and impulsively she reached out and touched the stubble-shadowed curve of his jaw. 'Thank you for changing your mind.'

'You changed my mind.'

She had? For a moment she was going to ask him how, but then she stopped herself. Strangers in bars didn't get to ask those kinds of questions.

'I'm glad.' She bit her lip. 'Do you think I could change it again? Because there's a beautiful John Hoyland that would work perfectly with the Freud. And a Damien Hirst I think you'd love.'

They stayed. And bought not just the Hoyland and the Hirst she'd mentioned, but another Hirst and a vivid yellow canvas by Maria Azzurri.

As they walked out into the warm early evening, she glanced past him, expecting to see the limo but there was no big car idling alongside the pavement.

'I thought we might go out to dinner,' Dante said quietly. 'Just something simple.'

In the past, 'simple' would have meant pizza, or a bowl of saffron-tinted risotto at a local *trattoria*.

Today, Dante's idea of something simple was a table in the two-Michelin-starred restaurant Locanda Luzzi, owned by chef of the moment Enrico Luzzi. No more than twenty diners could fit in the minimalist room, and as well as beautifully balanced dishes the service was the perfect ratio of discretion and professionalism.

'I thought there was some crazy long waiting list for dinner reservations here,' she said as they sat down next to the famous glass wall that opened on to the courtyard of a historic *palazzo*.

He held her gaze and she made a mock awe-struck face. 'Oh, this is one of your many assets.'

Not her favourite one, she thought, a pulse of heat beating across her skin as he nodded slowly.

'Rico was working in another restaurant I own. He impressed me, so I set him up in this place.'

She glanced assessingly around the dining room. 'So this is what? Money on a plate?'

He laughed, and her body seemed to fold in on itself as he reached across the table and caught her hand, his thumb brushing the underside of her wrist.

'I deserve that.'

'Yes, you do.' She smiled. 'It's okay. Your secret is safe with me,' she said softly.

She felt his fingers flex against her skin. His face stilled. 'My secret?'

Glancing over her shoulder, she lowered her voice conspiratorially. 'I know your art collection is actually about the art, not its market value.'

He held her gaze, and then his face shifted and the tension she hadn't fully registered until then faded as he smiled slowly. 'And that's down to you. You made me connect with it in a way I would never have imagined I could.'

A warm golden glow was wrapping around her skin and a feeling of intense happiness rose up inside her. 'My—'

She'd almost said *my grandfather* but stopped herself just in time. Why make it personal? Her grandfather wasn't a part of this, and she didn't want him to be. In fact, she needed to keep him and Dante separate. Her relationship with Dante was pared down to the bones of sex and money. Her grandfather was everything else.

'Your what?' Dante prompted.

She glanced over at him, grateful for the distraction. 'My belief is that you don't own a collection just by looking and appreciating. You have to feel it. You have to feel saudade, you know… You have to be dizzy with longing.'

His eyes locked with hers. 'I think I can do that,' he said softly.

The nearness of his clear grey eyes overwhelmed her, and for a moment she forgot what they were talking about. She forgot that they were in a restaurant with other diners. Suddenly there was just him, Dante King, the man with the sweetest smile and eyes like flames.

'Are you hungry?'

When she nodded, dumbly, he summoned the waiter with a brief nod of his dark head.

'Then let's order.'

Squashing a stray thought about how easy this was—talking, teasing, spending time with him—she glanced down at the menu. 'What do you normally have?'

There was a pause. 'I don't normally have anything. This is the first time I've been here,' he said finally. 'In fact, this is the first time I've been back to Milan since... Well, since we broke up.'

She blinked, her heart squeezing at his words as the waiter took their orders. But she was reading too much into it. Dante's career had not just taken off after they'd split—it had turned him overnight into a member of the richest one percent of people on the planet, with offices and homes all over the world.

'You've been very busy,' she said carefully.

'Signor King?'

The waiter had returned with their pasta and she turned, eager to be distracted from the sudden tension between them. Her eyes widened. 'Champagne?'

'Of course. We have something to celebrate.'

We again.

She ignored the twitch of her pulse and smiled as the waiter popped the cork discreetly. 'I'm glad you think so.' She held out her glass, smiling. 'Congratulations! You have the makings of a very fine collection.'

'Once again, that's thanks to you.'

His dark gaze settled on her face and she took a sip of champagne, lifting the glass to hide the sudden flush in her cheeks.

'You were right. You are very good at your job.'

Dante wasn't smiling, but there was a softness in his eyes that made her heart beat loudly for no reason. Watching him pick up his fork, expertly twirling it in his spaghetti before lifting it to his mouth, she said, 'I should be. I've been going to auctions since I was a child. In fact, I won my first auction when I was seven.'

Ignoring the urgent little voice at the back of her brain, telling her to change the subject, she felt her heart lurch, remembering her excitement. It had been a Gustave Doré woodcut of Cinderella for an unpublished volume of fairy tales. Now it was the only remaining picture in her bedroom at Ashburnham.

'Did your parents take you?' he asked.

She shook her head, her insides tightening with a panic she could neither explain nor stop. 'They both hate art.'

Although her father wasn't averse to taking it and selling it off when he needed the money.

His eyes were studying her face, considering her answer, and to stop the next inevitable question she said quickly, 'My grandparents used to take me, and then...' She hesitated, feeling a familiar ache spread inside her. 'And then, after my grandmother died, my grandfather took me on his own. It gave us both something to do.'

She'd said it too quickly. It had sounded harsh.

'When did she die?'

'When I was eight.' Her hands shook as she tried to cut up her chicken and she felt the exhilaration of winning the auctions ooze away. Talking about her parents was one thing, but she didn't trust herself to talk about Edward without crying.

'So your grandfather raised you? He took care of you?'

She nodded. And now he needed her to take care of him, and soon he wouldn't even know who she was. She would be lost to him and he to her.

It wouldn't be the first time she had been cut out of the life of someone she loved, but her grandfather was the first person who'd loved her back. And still loved her—even though dementia was destroying his brain.

She could feel her composure slipping, and suddenly she wished that they had just gone back to the villa. There, the rules of their arrangement felt clearer, somehow. They ate, and worked, and while they ate and worked they looked at one another. And when looking wasn't enough they went upstairs and had sex. Up until now they had been careful not to extend their conversation beyond what happened in the bedroom.

'Talitha?'

Dante was looking at her intently, and she had a sudden hysterical urge to laugh. All the time they'd been together she had wanted to know what he was thinking and feeling. Was this how he'd felt then? Cornered and exposed and alone?

But she knew he had never felt like that—because Dante didn't understand fear or failure. If something got in his way, then he found a way to eliminate it from his life. That was, after all, why he had suggested this lunatic arrangement with the two of them pretending to be strangers.

And she had gone along with it.

'Yes. He took care of me,' she said, in a voice that trembled slightly. 'So what? I know your family is cookie-cutter-perfect, but it's not a big deal.'

'I didn't say it was.'

'Then can we please change the subject?'

His eyes narrowed. 'What would you like to talk about?'

The easy intimacy they'd had moments earlier was fading, but she didn't care. In fact, she welcomed the edge of anger in his voice.

'Actually, I don't want to talk to you about anything, Dante. You and me—that's not what we're about, remember? We're just two strangers from a bar having sex.'

The dining room was suddenly very quiet.

Dante held her gaze. 'In that case, I think we'll skip dessert.' Eyes still resting on hers, he signalled to the waiter. *'Il conto, per favore.'*

The flight home was completely silent.

When they reached the villa she didn't wait for the driver, but yanked open the car door herself and ran lightly up the steps into the house.

Dante caught up with her outside her bedroom. 'What the hell are you playing at? Embarrassing me in a restaurant I own.'

She spun round to face him, her eyes wide with fury.

'I'm sorry if I embarrassed you, Dante. But if that's all you're worried about then your worries are over.'

'Cazzo!' He swore explosively. 'What are you talking about now?'

'I'm talking about *this*—this version of us. It's ugly and dishonest and wrong, and I don't want to do it anymore.' Suddenly she was fighting the beating of her heart, and she heard herself say hoarsely, 'The site visit is done and so are we. I'm going home tomorrow.'

And before he could open his mouth she slammed the door in his face.

CHAPTER EIGHT

As HE HEARD the key turn in the lock, Dante stared at the door in stunned silence, fury and frustration dancing across his skin like flames across a forest floor.

His head was spinning.

It made no sense, her turning on him like that.

He had been unsure about the trip right up until the moment he'd invited Talitha. It hadn't just been his dislike of public places. He liked this new understanding between them, and he'd childishly feared that it would somehow break the spell between them if they went outside the villa's protective charm and ventured into the real world.

But they had spent a perfect day together, reaching for one another as the first grainy light of dawn slipped into the bedroom, then flying to Milan after lunch for the auction.

He breathed out shakily. In truth, he had barely registered any of the artworks being carried in and out of the room. He had been too busy watching Talitha, drawn to the flush of pink colouring her cheeks, the glitter of excitement in her eyes and the curves of her body in that stunning Chinoiserie dress.

She'd looked beautiful—so beautiful that he'd kept forgetting to breathe. And everything had seemed easy between them—easier than it had ever been in Milan before, when he'd been on edge the entire time, thinking about how she would react if and when he told her the truth about his childhood and his family.

Only now she was the one holding back. He was here, locked out of her life—not just metaphorically, but literally—and tomorrow she would go back to England.

His chest tightened. He had deliberately avoided confronting the issue of her leaving, letting each day pass, choosing not to keep a tally.

It shouldn't matter. He shouldn't care. He shouldn't have even felt the need to follow her upstairs.

But he hadn't been able to stop himself from going after her. Or standing here like some thwarted Romeo outside her door. Because he was angry, he told himself quickly, and that was Talitha's fault. She was the one who had provoked the fight, even though she'd told him she didn't want to fight any more.

Turning away from her door, he caught sight of the moon through the landing window and felt his heartbeat slow as he walked towards it.

That wasn't the only reason he'd followed her. This time there had been a brittleness to her anger—a pain that went deeper than their stupid argument in the restaurant. He'd heard it in her voice. More importantly, she'd heard it too, and that was why she had provoked a fight, so she could hide behind her rage.

He sat down on the window seat and let his head fall back against the wall.

Only what was she hiding?

He didn't know how long he sat there, or when he dozed off, but he jerked awake with the sudden, immediate knowledge that he was not alone.

'Dante?'

Talitha was standing beside him, her face pale in the moonlight, her pupils wide like a startled doe. She was barefoot, but she was still wearing the beautiful black Chinoiserie dress from earlier.

'What are you doing?' she asked.

He shifted, stretching out the crick in his neck. 'I guess I must have fallen asleep.'

She stared at him in silence. 'Why are you sleeping out here?' she said at last.

His eyes rested on her face. She sounded calm, but he could tell from the way her shoulders rose and fell that she was fighting to stay on top of her breathing.

He felt his stomach knot.

Talitha wasn't the only one hiding herself. He was hiding too. He had heard how upset she was, but chosen to ignore it, telling himself that he hadn't signed on for her pain.

The knot in his stomach tightened.

His entire life he had been ashamed of who he was. But this was the first time that he'd felt more ashamed of who he was now than where he had come from, and shock and self-disgust made him do something he hadn't been intending to do.

He told her the truth.

'I didn't want to go to bed on my own. I like holding you when I sleep.'

She looked past him at the moon, one arm curled across her stomach as if she had a pain there. He couldn't blame her for choosing the moon over him. The moon hadn't blackmailed her into coming here. Or offered up some role-play in lieu of an actual honest conversation.

'I'm sorry, Talitha,' he said quietly. 'I keep hurting you and I don't want to.'

'That's not true.' She shook her head. 'Everything you've done has been to hurt me, to punish me for leaving you in Milan.'

'In the beginning, yes,' he admitted. 'I was angry. But I'm not angry with you now. I'm angry with myself. For trapping you into doing something you didn't want to do.'

She looked down at her tightly linked hands. 'You didn't trap me into having sex with you. I wanted to. I still do. I thought I could put the past to one side. It's not like I haven't done it so many times before. Only—' She stopped for a moment and swallowed, 'I don't know why, but I can't do it with you.'

She still wasn't looking at him, but through the curving arc of her hair he saw a tear slip down her cheek.

'Talitha...'

In the space of a heartbeat Dante stood up and

wrapped his arms around her. A sob caught in her throat and she stiffened against him, and then he felt her body slacken, her face distorting as she dissolved into tears.

His throat squeezed tight. He had never seen Talitha cry before, and hearing her pain almost broke him in two. Cupping the back of her head with his hand, he pressed her closer, gently stroking her back. Gradually her sobs subsided and, still holding her close, he dropped down on the window seat and pulled her onto his lap.

For a long time he sat there, cradling her against him, until finally she breathed out shakily. 'I'm sorry about before. In the restaurant.'

'You don't need to apologise, *ciccia*.' His fingers tightened against her back. The pain he had been trying to avoid was eating him up inside. 'I deserved everything you said and more. You were right. I didn't think it through. I was just so desperate for it not to be a one-off.'

'I know, and I understand—I do. Desperation makes people do stupid things.'

Her voice sounded a long way away from him and, watching her hands clench in her lap, he thought back to what she had just said a moment earlier, about putting the past to one side many times before.

'Look, Talitha, I can completely understand why you wouldn't trust me,' he said carefully, knowing that he was treading on sensitive ground. 'I wasn't and I haven't been there for you.' He stared down at the top of her head, willing her to trust him, to give him a chance. 'But I'm here now.'

His breath twisted in his throat. How could he ask her to trust him? He had never once been honest with her about his own past, his fears, his motives. But, blanking his mind to the hypocrisy of his words, he brushed his lips against her hair.

'I'm here, and I'm not going anywhere.'

But Talitha was still looking down at her hands, and he knew with a sharp, accusatory sting of pain that he had failed her again.

He felt suddenly bone-tired and, glancing out of the window, saw that the sky was growing lighter. She must be exhausted too.

He was about to suggest that she go to bed when she said quietly, 'After my parents left, I was desperate for them to come back for me. One day my mother just turned up, out of the blue.'

She was telling it like a story, but he already knew from the stress in her voice that it would be one without a happy ending.

'She told me she wanted me to live with her and that it was all worked out. She just needed me to talk to my father first, about her spousal maintenance. Sometimes it would be my father who got in touch. Once he came to collect me only instead he took a couple of paintings and left me behind. It was always the same promises— just with different conditions attached.'

Talitha looked up at him then, and the hurt in her eyes took his breath away.

'But they didn't keep their promises.'

He clenched his teeth. *Any more than I did*, he thought.

She shook her head. 'At the last minute there would always be some reason why it couldn't happen, and I made excuses for them. I wouldn't let go. I just kept giving them another chance. And then another. I thought that if I met them halfway—usually more than halfway—then I could make it work.'

He heard her swallow.

'And then I met you. I wasn't looking for a husband. I wasn't even looking for a lover. But I couldn't not be with you. I thought it was just sex, only then I realised I was in love with you.'

She bit into her lip.

'And I was so happy, but I was also terrified. I didn't think you would love me…that I was lovable. That's why I proposed. So that there would be something more than just me tying us together. Only then you went back to America without me, and I knew nothing would ever be enough.'

He hated the pain in her voice—hated that he had contributed to that pain. 'I'm sorry, Talitha.'

'It doesn't matter now. I just want you to understand why I did what I did.'

He understood everything. Her parents had made false promises, put their needs above hers, and he had done the same. And now he was doing it again. Suggesting they act like strangers in a bar, even though they had once been engaged to one another.

'Do your parents know what they did to you?' he asked.

For a moment he thought he'd pressed too hard against the bruise, but then she shook her head again.

'But what I said before, about not fitting in with their lives, that's wrong. They don't fit into mine. Not anymore. It's their fault we almost lost Ashburnham, and I will never forgive them for that.'

He cleared his throat. 'You've put that right.'

'No, you've put it right. But there's some things I can't put right. Like how I treated my grandfather.' Her voice wavered. 'Whenever they turned up or called me I would forget all about him.' Her eyes were filled with tears. 'Even though he was always there for me.'

His hand stilled against her back. Like his adopted parents had been there for him. They were still the only people he truly trusted. They alone knew the damaged, partial person he had once been, and they loved him anyway.

He cleared his throat. 'You're his granddaughter; he loves you.'

'And I love him. He's been so much more than a grandfather. He's been a parent and a mentor. He taught me about art and beauty and he made me feel safe. He gave me love and encouragement and a home.' Her mouth was trembling. 'Back in London you said that people like me care about having a perfect shopfront, but I would have sold Ashburnham years ago if I could. Only I can't.'

Picking up her hand, he gave it a squeeze. 'There are people who can take care of that for you,' he said gently. 'You wouldn't need to get involved.'

'It's not that.'

She shook her head, and again he saw the sheen of tears in her eyes.

'I can't sell it because it's not just my home, it's my grandfather's too. It's the only one he's ever known. Only soon he won't know it at all. Soon he might not even know me. Because...' She hesitated. 'Because he's got dementia.'

Dante stared down at her in shock. He felt as if someone had pushed a knife into his chest.

'Some days he's fine and then others...' Her face quivered. 'He gets so confused and scared. I think probably it was happening some time before I noticed, but I thought it was just him getting old. And then he had a car accident on the estate, just after I got back from Milan.'

She took a deep breath.

'That's why I didn't get to tell Ned that I couldn't marry him. Grandpa wasn't badly hurt, but when the doctor talked to him he didn't even know what a steering wheel was. It was like he'd forgotten.'

Her voice wobbled a little, and Dante felt the knife in his chest twist.

'And now it's just getting worse, and I know I can't stop it, but I'm not going to let anyone push him out of his home. I don't care who it is or what they threaten.'

'Shh...it's okay.' Grabbing her arms, he held her firmly, his eyes fixed on hers. 'Nobody is going to push him out of his home, *ciccia*. Not now. Not ever.'

Scooping Talitha into his arms, he carried her into her bedroom, undressed her and helped her into her pyjamas.

'Into bed,' he ordered. He tucked the sheet around her body and, leaning over her, kissed her gently. 'I'll see you in the morning.'

Her hand caught his wrist. 'I thought you liked holding me while you slept,' she murmured.

'I do.'

Her eyelashes fluttered against the smooth curve of her cheekbone. 'I like it too.'

As he slid in beside her she fell asleep immediately. Gazing down at her face, Dante felt as if he would never sleep again.

Not that he deserved to.

He had behaved appallingly. Intent on obliterating both her and that sense of unfinished business between them, he had happily used the part she'd played in their shared past to justify his actions, never once stopping to question anything.

Only he'd been wrong about so much.

And instead of freeing himself from those last hints of doubt he was veering off course, straying into new and uncharted territory where Talitha was no longer the spoiled, self-centred darling of the London social scene he'd always imagined her to be.

On the contrary—he knew now that she had overcome her parents' rejection to become a strong, successful woman in her own right. And, far from being self-centred, she was caring for the man who had raised her, fighting her grandfather's corner with the ferocity of a tigress.

He stared down at her in the darkness. Her breathing was so soft and her hair was a swirling golden teardrop against the pillow.

He wanted her.

He wanted her even more now than he had that first night they'd met. Even more terrifyingly, he didn't just want her body. He wanted to see her smile, wanted to *make* her smile, to make her happy.

His jaw tightened. First, though, he was going to have to persuade her not to go back to England...

Stepping out of the shower, Talitha wrapped a towel around her body, grabbed another from the pile, and began drying her hair.

At least that was what her hands were doing.

Her head, though, was replaying what had happened last night, from the moment Dante had caught up with her outside her room to when he'd climbed into bed beside her and held her as she fell asleep.

She had woken to find herself alone, and her heart had filled with a kind of yearning surge as she'd remembered the press of his body and the gentle caress of his hand as he stroked her hair.

In the restaurant she had felt so trapped. Not just by the present, and the mess she had made of coming to Italy with Dante, but by the memory of all those times when she'd believed her parents' lies.

She had never told anyone before. Obviously her grandfather knew, but she had been too ashamed to admit it to other people. Too scared that she might draw attention to whatever it was that her parents had seen in her that had made them walk away.

And she wouldn't have told Dante last night, only the walls had been closing in on her. Needing space and fresh air, she'd decided to go downstairs and sit on the terrace. And when she'd unlocked the door he had been there, his big body wedged uncomfortably on the window seat, like a faithful hound.

Like Bluebell, in fact, who sat and steadfastly watched the front door whenever her grandfather left the house without her.

It had caught her off guard, so that before she'd been able to stop herself she had walked over to him—and then, of course, he'd woken up.

Her heart skipped. Dante had been sweet and patient and gentle in a way that had reminded her so much of her grandfather she didn't know now why she had been worried about telling him the truth. What she did know was that she might have unlocked the door to her bedroom, but Dante had unlocked the door to her past.

And now her secrets were free. Like caged birds they had simply taken flight. And she felt calm, happy and whole in a way that she hadn't for weeks…maybe months.

Frowning, she bit her lip. *Make that years.*

'You're up.'

She turned, her heartbeat faltering. With most people, after your brain had processed and memorised their features, you stopped looking, but with Dante the more she looked at him, the more there was to enchant her.

'Yes. I was just about to get dressed—' She broke off, her gaze following his as it panned slowly around the empty wardrobe and shelves. 'Only I forgot I packed everything last night.'

In her pain and despair she had been like a mindless force of nature—a whirlwind snatching up neatly folded T-shirts and shorts, blindly tugging dresses from their hangers and tossing them into her suitcase.

There was a short silence, and then he reached out and touched her cheek gently. 'Please stay. I know you need to go home, but could we just have this last day together? There's something I'd like to do with you today. Somewhere I'd like to take you.'

Talitha stared at him, her heart thudding unevenly. Inside her head she could see her and Dante moving as one, their bodies coalescing as day became night, the hazy afternoon sunshine shifting into liquid moonlight and then back into a grainy dawn, like in those time-lapse films used in nature programmes on TV.

And then she thought back to the moment in the restaurant when she had felt so cornered and diminished.

As if he could read her mind, Dante shook his head. 'I don't mean like before. I know that isn't what you want, and I don't want it either. I don't think it can work if we're not ourselves. The real you and me.'

The real you and me.

In the aftermath of her confession there seemed to be poetry in his words. And a finality, she thought, her chest tensing at the thought that today would be her last day here with Dante.

'The real you and me, but better,' she said slowly, pushing aside the flutter of pain and sadness. 'Now everything is straight between us and there's no more secrets or lies like there was before.'

Something shifted in his eyes—or she thought it did. But when she looked again it was gone and he was nodding slowly, his thumb caressing her cheek in a way that made her tremble inside.

'No more secrets or lies,' he agreed.

'So what is it? What are we doing today?'

'I have a horse running in the Palio, and I would really like you to come and watch the race with me.'

She felt her skin contract as his thumb brushed against the corner of her mouth.

'I thought you might bring me luck,' he said.

The Palio. She had heard of it, but only half believed it was real. A horse race in the centre of Siena? How was that even possible?

'I'd love that,' she said quickly.

His lips curved into one those minute almost-smiles. 'Just don't tell anyone I called it a race. It's actually the most intense, lawless, crazy ninety-second contest of horsepower and pride on the planet.'

She reached up and touched his face, her fingers moving from the stubble of his jaw to the silken softness of his hair. 'It sounds right up my street,' she teased. 'What time do we need to be there?'

'Some time in the afternoon.'

'So I don't need to get dressed just yet?' she said softly, feeling a pulse starting between her thighs as his pupils flared.

'Not yet, no.'

'In that case…' She unhooked the towel and let it

fall to the floor. Heard him suck in a breath and felt her nipples tighten in anticipation.

There was a thrill in seeing him so aroused, knowing she had the power to arouse him. And, holding his gaze, she let her hand slip down her naked body to the curls between her thighs.

His eyes hardened, grew hotter, and then he leaned forward and kissed her hard—a searing, open-mouthed kiss of hunger and possession. And then, still kissing her, he picked her up and carried her back into the bedroom.

Tilting his head back, Dante gazed up at the vaulted star-spangled ceiling of the Santa Maria Assunta, his throat tightening. The last time he had been here was as a child, with his new adoptive parents Connie and Robert King. They had held his hands in theirs—not so tightly that it hurt, but tightly enough for him to know that they would notice and care if he was not there.

It had been an epiphany—an understanding of what a parent could be. What a parent *should* be. Even now, more than two decades later, he could still remember his relief and gratitude that they had found him, and he would associate that feeling of being found with this city for ever. It was the main reason he had chosen to buy a home here.

Only it was Talitha's hand in his now, and he felt a rush of thankfulness that she had stayed, and that she was here with him now, and that everything was good between them.

Something twisted inside him. But what exactly did he mean by 'good'?

'The real you and me, but better.'

That was what Talitha thought—what he had let her think. But he had lied. The real Dante was a liar and a coward. And that was why he had decided this morning as she'd slept to ask her to the Palio.

He couldn't tell her the truth. But this was as close as he could get. He was peeling back a layer, sharing a part of himself that had nothing to do with work or his carefully curated image.

'Isn't it beautiful?'

He felt Talitha's fingers tighten around his and, glancing down at her face, saw that there were tears in her eyes. He nodded, but for him nothing could compare with her beauty. And he didn't just mean the beauty of her bones, but something deeper and more intrinsic—a sweetness and a strength that was more dazzling than any of the cathedral's luminous frescoes or the paintings that would soon be hanging in his home.

She bit her lip. Her eyes were soft and hazy, like the sky at dawn. 'Do we have time to go round and look at everything again?' she asked.

Drawing her against him, he kissed her softly. 'We have all the time in the world.'

They ate lunch at a small *trattoria* in Banchi di Sopra. While they ate, Dante told Talitha about the Palio.

'It's actually two races. One in July and one in August.' Picking up his bread, he tore off a piece. 'It dates back to the thirteenth century—only then they used to race buffaloes.'

She screwed up her face. 'That sounds like a terrifying idea. Does *palio* mean buffalo, then?'

'Good guess, but no.' He smiled. 'It means banner. The race is held to honour the Virgin Mary, and the *contrada* who wins the race gets the banner painted with her image.'

'And the *contrada* is the jockey?'

Still smiling, he shook his head. 'A *contrada* is a district of the city. My horse is racing for Aquila— the Eagle—but Siena has seventeen districts in total, and they have an all-consuming on-going rivalry. It all comes to a head at the Palio. Bribery is rife, and horses have been drugged and jockeys kidnapped. But the race is the most dangerous part. Every year jockeys get hurt—horses too.'

She bit her lip. 'Aren't you worried your horse will get hurt?'

Catching sight of her expression, he picked up her hand and pressed it against his mouth. 'A little. But he's compact and very fast—a real *piazzaiolo*. And there's a saying in Siena: *il Palio è vita*. The Palio is life. It might only last ninety seconds, but it's talked about all year, and it's a great honour to have a horse chosen.'

Leaning across the table, she touched his face. 'You deserve it,' she said softly.

His eyes found hers. 'For what?'

'You're a good man.' She took a breath. 'Paying off the loan doesn't just get the bank off my back, it means my grandfather can keep his home, and I'll never forget that, so thank you.'

Her words echoed inside his head as they made their way through the clogged streets. If concealing the truth from Talitha already made him feel shabby, it was nothing to how he had felt when she looked up at him with those huge shining eyes.

And it wasn't just guilt and self-loathing picking at him. There was something final in what she'd said—a kind of unspoken goodbye—so that even though he knew today was their last together, it made it much more real.

He had a sudden urge to pull her away from the surging crowds and tell her that he was sorry, ask her to forgive him.

'What is it?' Talitha was looking up at him, and her excitement of earlier was tinged with uncertainty. 'Is everything okay?'

He felt a spasm of guilt. This was her day. He was not going to ruin it by— By what? Asking her to stay? Offering something insultingly partial and secondrate like he had before? That wasn't going to happen.

'I'd forgotten how many people there'd be,' he lied.

'Will we be able to get in?' she said anxiously.

Dante nodded. 'Some friends of my parents—Gianni and Angela—live in one of the houses in the Piazza del Campo. They've invited us to watch the race with them.'

The Continis were actually two of his parents' oldest friends, and up until a few days ago he wouldn't have considered letting Talitha meet them. But today was an exception. He wanted to share this small part of his life with her. And it wasn't going to be a quiet dinner, with lots of questions and reminiscences. The Palio was a theatrical onslaught on the senses. With so much going on there would be no time for much more than pleasantries.

He ran his hand gently down her arm. 'You don't mind, do you? It's just a bit of an endurance test doing it any other way, what with the crowds and the heat.'

Momentarily lost for words, Talitha shook her head. She was stunned. Had Dante really just said that he was taking her to meet some friends of his parents?

Her heart pounded in her throat. She had thought he was just taking her out for the day, but this was different: this was personal. He was letting her into his world. The same world he had excluded her from all those years ago. And not begrudgingly or by chance. He had invited her. It was his choice.

'I don't mind at all,' she said quickly.

By the time they reached the Continis' house her pulse was racing. With such short notice she had no expectations, and yet as soon as she met them she couldn't imagine them being any other way. They were almost exactly her idea of the archetypal Italian *nonni*.

They were sweetly excited to meet her, and judging by the flurry of emotional Italian accompanied by so many kisses she lost count, they both doted on Dante.

'Talitha…such a pretty name. You must sit here, in the shade,' Angela said, glancing anxiously up at the sun as she led Talitha onto the balcony. 'Dante, go with

Gianni and get some water,' she ordered. '*Una caraffa.* It is already so hot.'

It was blisteringly hot and, glancing down at the boiling sea of spectators crushed into the *conca* in the centre of the track, Talitha was grateful to be up so high, where there was at least a whisper of a breeze.

'Thank you so much for inviting me. It's a wonderful view. Like having a box at the opera.'

'Thank you for bringing Dante.' Angela beamed at her. 'Always we ask him to come, but he is so busy with work. This is the first year he comes—and with such a beautiful girl. I cannot wait to tell Connie. She will be so happy.'

Talitha felt a giddiness that had nothing to do with the heat or the height of the balcony. All she really knew about his background was that he had emigrated to America from Italy when he was a child. Now, after all this time, to suddenly meet someone who knew Dante and his family was like waking up after a long journey to discover she had finally reached a longed-for destination.

There were so many questions she wanted to ask, but before she had a chance to ask any of them Dante and Gianni returned.

'This is the Corteo Historico,' Dante said softly as he sat down beside her, his body brushing against hers.

Down in the square, carts pulled by oxen and hundreds of people in historical costumes, many on horseback, some drumming, some waving flags, began to walk slowly around the track.

'It's incredible,' she whispered, twisting to look at

him. 'Imagine having all this on your doorstep. No wonder you wanted to live here. Or do you have a more personal connection to the area?'

She wasn't sure how he would react, but after a moment he nodded slowly. 'Yes, I do. This is where my family is from.'

The sun dipped lower, and then the pigeons on the nearby roofs scattered into the sky as the boom of a cannon filled the air. Abruptly the crowd grew quiet as the jockeys in their brightly coloured clothes rode into the *piazza*, the horses jostling one another, skittering backwards and rearing up.

Talitha turned to Dante. 'They don't have saddles.'

He shook his head. 'Don't worry. They have helmets and—' he pointed towards the mattresses piled against the walls of the houses '—there are some safety measures.'

She nodded. 'So which one is yours?'

'The jockey in yellow on the grey horse. The jockey is Luigi Sarratorre. They call him La Patella—the Limpet—and the horse's name is Argento Vivo.'

He had barely finished speaking when the rope dropped and they were off. The crowd roared. There was a clattering blur of hooves and colour and then a furious, scrambling rush. Two horses went crashing into the mattresses at the Curva di San Martino, losing their riders in the process, but the Limpet clung on.

Now they surged round a hairpin corner, galloping with power and purpose. Talitha could hardly breathe. It was the last lap. Everyone was standing and screaming, including her, as the rider in yellow nudged his horse on, and as he crossed the finishing line the *piazza* erupted. People were hurling themselves onto the track, crying, clutching one another, and she was clutching Dante.

His eyes were blazing.

'You won! You won!' Her voice was hoarse, and her heart felt as though it would burst. She found his mouth and kissed him fiercely. 'You won the Palio.'

Nodding slowly, almost as if he didn't believe it, he reeled her in towards him. 'How could I lose?' he said softly. 'You're my lucky charm. When I'm with you, everything is right.'

She knew he was talking about the race but, caught in the shared intensity of his triumph, she looked up at him, dizzy with heat and happiness and love.

Love.

Her pulse was pounding hard in her head and she felt her fingers slip against his skin. She couldn't be in love. But she knew that she was.

It was why she hadn't been able even to think about seeing another man. And why she had agreed to come to Siena. She loved him, had never stopped loving him, and accepting that filled her with an inviolable calmness that was at odds with the wild delirium around her.

Her longing to tell him was so powerful she felt almost sick, but there was no time. Dante was already pulling her back into the house and down the stairs into the street, and now they were joining the river of people heading uphill to the Duomo.

CHAPTER NINE

It was her second visit of the day to the cathedral, and it seemed impossible to Talitha that so much could have changed in such a short time. Not outwardly—although, given the heat and the amount of shouting she had done, that too. But it was a change she felt in herself…in her heart.

Just a few hours ago the cathedral had been still and silent, and she had been dazzled by the serene beauty of the eight-hundred-year-old building. Now it was filled with a jubilant crowd from the Aquila *contrada*, all singing thunderously and waving their yellow and black flags, and the air was thick with heat and sweat and triumph.

Her senses were on overload, and yet she was conscious only of Dante's muscular body, curving protectively around hers. But had anything changed for him?

At that moment the winning jockey was carried into the nave on the shoulders of several young men, and the crowd sang a 'Te Deum' as he received a blessing from the Archbishop.

Then it was over, and she and Dante made their way

out into the street hand in hand. When an old man with a tear-stained face stepped forward and clapped him on the back she made herself ignore how it felt almost like a wedding.

Turning, she looked up at Dante and smiled. 'So, what happens now?'

'We celebrate,' he said softly.

They met Angela and Gianni for a huge dinner in the Aquila district's main square. At night the city was magical, and it was a loud, boisterous evening, with plenty of good food and wine, all accompanied by the smell and smoke of firecrackers and songs and drumming from the still celebrating *contrada*.

As he was the winning *cavallaio* a lot of people wanted to talk to Dante, and when yet another group of men came up to congratulate him she turned to Angela and said, 'Everyone is so happy. I can't think of anything in England when people would be so full of joy. A royal wedding, maybe…'

Angela smiled. 'The Palio is more than a race,' she said, her words echoing Dante's. 'It is the day when the city stops to scream and cry and cheer. Mostly scream and cry.' She patted Talitha on the hand. 'But today we cheer, so I think you must come back next year. The last two times Dante's horse comes second.'

Talitha laughed. 'At least it didn't come last.'

As she shook her head, Angela made one of those hand gestures that Italians were so fond of. 'In the Palio, the losing horse is not the one that comes in last, but the one that finishes in second place. But this year we won. *He* won.' Leaning forward, she whispered, 'Don't worry, *mia cara*! It took me a long time too.'

Talitha frowned. 'What did?'

'To understand why the Palio matters so much. But after fifteen years I know now that the people of this city belong to their *contrada* first, then to Siena, and lastly to Italy.'

Talitha stared at her in confusion, the memory of her conversation with Dante quivering in her mind. 'You're not from Siena?'

Angela shook her head. 'No, no, no. We moved here for Gianni's job, but we were both born and grew up in Naples. Like Connie. And of course Dante.' Her face softened. 'I lived on the same street as Connie and went to the same school. We saw each other every day until she moved to America with Robert.'

It was suddenly difficult for Talitha to breathe, to sit up straight. What had started as an itch beneath her skin—the kind that was so tiny it was impossible to decide if it was even real—was now a prickling sense of panic spreading over her skin.

She tried to think of some sensible, reassuring explanation. There must be a mistake. Angela spoke very good English, but maybe something had got lost in translation. Probably they would laugh later at the mix-up.

Or perhaps she had misunderstood what Dante had said to her.

Her throat tightened. But she knew that she hadn't.

There was a huge cheer from the other end of the table, and as Angela glanced over her shoulder Talitha picked up her glass clumsily and drank her wine. But no amount of wine could change the facts.

Dante had told her that his family was from Siena.

Why would anyone lie about where they came from?

The question remained unanswered throughout the speeches and the toasts that followed. In time with the ragged thud of her heartbeat, Talitha went through the pantomime of smiling and raising her glass and cheering, but she barely registered anything other than the ache of confusion and sadness in her chest.

In the car on the way home she had to look away from him. She would have been hurt at any time, but to find out today, after they'd seemed so close, made her feel ill. When they reached the villa she didn't go upstairs, but went straight to the kitchen and filled a glass with cold water from the tap.

'Is everything okay?'

Dante's hand against her back felt cool and firm, and she could hear the concern in his voice. More than anything she wished that she could just rewind the last hour of her life—go back in time to when she had let hope flower in her heart, before Angela had snatched off her rose-tinted glasses.

If only she could just pretend.

But there had already been too much pretending.

She shook her head slowly. 'No, it's not. But I can't blame anyone but myself.'

There was a long silence. 'You're going to have to help me, Talitha. I really don't know what you're talking about,' he said finally.

'Help you?' She lifted her eyes 'Of course. I mean,

that's what we were always about. Me helping you. Why should this be any different? After all, nothing else has changed, even though you stood there this morning and told me that you wanted today to be about to be the "real" me and you.'

His expression didn't change, but she felt his mood shift like scenery behind the curtains at a play.

'I meant what I said,' he told her.

'And I believed you,' she scoffed. 'I thought everything was straight between us. You said there would be no more secrets or lies. So why did you tell me your family come from Siena when they don't?'

Saying it out loud made the numbness in her chest spread to her throat. It wasn't as if he had just lied about what his favourite colour was. And what made it worse was that only this morning she had poured out her heart to him.

'I don't understand—I don't understand why you wouldn't just tell me the truth.'

There was a longer silence this time, so long that she thought he wasn't going to answer, but then she heard him take a breath. 'And that's exactly why I didn't tell you.'

She felt her entire body tense. His voice sounded taut, as if he was fighting to get the words out, or maybe to hold them back.

'Because you wouldn't understand.'

Her heart was beating hard—so hard she could feel it pounding through her like the drumming in the *piazza*. Only it was beating in panic, not triumph.

'Understand what?'

He didn't say anything, and she reached out and touched his arm. It felt like stone, as if she was touching one of the statues in the garden. All the warmth and vitality, the fierce elation after the Palio, had drained out of him.

'I was born in Naples. But I didn't lie to you.'

She stared at him in confusion. His words made no sense, but she knew the answer to her question was hidden in them. Like those clues in the cryptic crosswords her grandfather had used to love so much.

Her thoughts scampered back to the beginning of the day, when they had both stood gazing up at the Duomo's star-encrusted ceiling. The trip had been his idea, and she'd thought it was for her benefit. Now, though, she knew without fully knowing why that she had been wrong.

'Did something happen in Siena? Something important?' she asked softly.

There was a longer silence.

'My parents brought me here on holiday. It was the first holiday I'd ever had. The first time I'd ever left Naples. The first time I'd been in a cathedral.'

'That's a lot of firsts.'

He nodded. 'It was also the first time I felt safe. Wanted. Loved.'

How could that be? He loved his parents. She was sure of that. In Milan he had talked to both his mother and father frequently, and although he'd spoken in Italian there had been a tenderness in his voice that was unmistakable.

'They held my hands the whole time. No one had

ever held my hands before.' He hesitated, a muscle flickering in his jaw, then, 'Except social workers or police officers. My parents barely noticed me. My biological parents, I mean. Not that they were around much. Most of the time they were in prison.'

She felt her legs wobble as the blood in her head rushed downwards.

Prison.

The word ricocheted around the silent kitchen like a bullet.

Taking a breath, she tried to keep her voice steady. 'Your parents were in prison?'

Leaning back against the counter, he nodded again. 'Not just my parents. The whole glorious Cannavaro clan. My brothers. My uncles. My cousins.' His mouth curved upwards into a slanting smile that hurt to look at. 'And me. Although I didn't actually commit any crime. I was born there. In the prison hospital.'

The pain wasn't just in his voice now. He was swathed in it like a shroud. Without thinking, she stepped forward and slid both arms around him, held him close, embracing his pain, absorbing it into her body.

'I'm so sorry, Dante. That's awful.'

His mouth twisted. 'I don't remember it. My aunt looked after me until my mother was released, and then I was basically in and out of care until I was five. Then the courts made an adoption order.'

How could she not have known about any of this? That first time they'd met in that bar she had sensed a vulnerability in him, but that, like everything else, had got lost in the heat of their passion. And then, after everything had fallen apart, she'd just thought she'd misread him from the off.

'Is that when you met Connie and Robert?'

Watching his face soften, she swallowed the tears rising in her throat.

'It took about six months for everything to be finalised, and then another six months for me to accept that it was real.'

'But you did. That day in the Duomo?' she said quietly.

He nodded. 'That was when I realised that they loved me. They'd seen me at my worst, when I was so angry and damaged and fragmented that I couldn't accept love. I just kept pushing them away, but they didn't let go. For me, that moment in the cathedral was when we became a family.'

And that was why he'd said what he had.

'I didn't mean to lie to you, Talitha.'

She felt his arms tighten around her.

'When we moved to the States it was like a new beginning. I had a different name, and nobody knew about my past. Most people didn't even know I was adopted, and that was how I wanted it. I couldn't imagine ever needing to tell anyone.'

'What do you mean?' She looked up at him, and he screwed up his face.

'I was pretty uncool as a kid. You know…skinny and short with braces.' His mouth curved minutely at the corners. 'Even more uncool, I was good at maths. I found it hard to make friends, and I didn't even talk to a girl until I went to college. My parents told me it would be different when I met the right woman, but I never did—until you.'

The right woman.

When I'm with you everything is right.

His words jostled inside her head and she felt a ripple of warmth skim across her skin, a bud of hope as he stared down at her.

'I couldn't believe it when you came over to me in that bar. I actually thought it was some kind of dare or a bet.'

'Is that why you were so quiet?'

He nodded. 'And I was shy.'

She bit her lip. 'Not *that* shy.'

His face stilled. 'I'd never done anything like that before. I'd never wanted to. I thought it would be just a one-night stand for you, and that you'd leave in the morning. Only you stayed.' Reaching out, he caressed her cheek. 'I was completely smitten, and I knew I should tell you about my past, but every time I thought about saying something I'd talk myself out of it. I kept thinking you'd call time, only you didn't, and by then we were getting serious, and I still hadn't told you, and it just got harder and harder to find the right time and the right words.'

Talitha bit down hard on the inside of her lip. She had felt the same way—felt the same fear, the same paralysing sense of inertia.

His eyes locked with hers. 'I know now that you would have understood, but back then I felt nobody could ever understand, because they only knew the latest version of me. When you proposed I made up my mind to tell you. Only then that man grabbed your bag, and it changed everything.'

She looked up at him as he paused. 'What changed?'

His grey eyes flickered past her to the darkness of the house. 'It all happened so fast. When I caught up with him I wasn't thinking straight. I wasn't thinking at all. I wanted to scare him, to hurt him—*really* hurt him—but I didn't. I punched the wall instead.'

Her chest tightened as she remembered his bloodied knuckles and the cut on his lip. 'He hurt you.'

Dante shook his head. 'You don't understand. I could feel it inside me—the anger and the violence and the chaos. And I knew that all of it had been for nothing. I'd changed my name, I'd changed continents, but I was still a Cannavaro. Instead of scaring him, I scared myself.' His voice cracked, and he struggled to speak. 'And I scared you.'

Looking up into his face, she felt as if her heart was going to burst. He looked wretched; she could almost see the shame eating at him. 'You didn't scare me, Dante. I was worried about you.'

He shook his head, his beautiful face contorting. 'I didn't want you to worry about me. I wanted you to be proud of me. Only how could I expect you to be proud of someone who was willing to beat a man to a pulp with his bare hands?'

'But you didn't.'

'I wanted to. And I didn't want to tie you to someone like that. Someone like my father and my brothers. But I knew that if I was with you I wouldn't be strong enough to end it. When my dad called about my mum's operation, it seemed like the perfect solution.'

Her heart plummeted. She had been right: he *had* been going to end it. The hope she had felt seconds earlier shrivelled inside her.

'Except it wasn't. The whole time I was there I couldn't stop thinking about you, and I realised that I couldn't not be with you.' He clenched his teeth. 'But I couldn't keep lying either, and that's when I knew that I had to prove to you that I wasn't like my family. If I was going to share my past, I knew that I had to give you a future worth having. I had an idea for a business... I just needed investment.'

'That's why you went and talked to Nick?' she whispered.

When he nodded, the tears she'd been holding back started to spill down her cheeks.

'Don't cry.' He smoothed her cheeks with trembling hands. 'Please don't cry. I don't ever want to make you cry.'

She couldn't look at him. If only she had been whole...if only she had been able to share her past instead of concealing it.

As if reading her mind, he shook his head. 'It's not your fault, Talitha. We both made mistakes.' Sliding his hands into her hair, he tilted her face up to his, forcing her to look at him. 'Everything happened so fast, and I don't think either of us were really ready for a serious relationship.'

And was he now?

She so badly wanted to ask him, but neither of them

was in a fit state to have that particular conversation. In fact, the time for talking was over.

'Let's go to bed,' she said quietly, as soon as she could trust her voice. And, taking his hand, she led him upstairs.

Without speaking, Dante closed the door and pulled her against him, their mouths fusing. His hands slid beneath her dress, moving past the silk, and they fell back onto the bed and made love with their clothes on, the heat of their hunger burning their skin through the fabric.

Dante woke up with a start, his heart pounding. He had been dreaming of the Palio, only in the dream he wasn't the owner but the jockey, and instead of there being only three laps, the race wouldn't end.

'What is it?' Talitha was looking at him anxiously, her beautiful face creased.

He drew her closer and kissed her softly on the lips. 'It was just a bad dream. I thought I'd lost the Palio again,' he lied.

As her face relaxed, he glanced down at their naked bodies. They had made love again and again, and each time they had taken another piece of clothing off. Neither of them had felt the need to talk. And now that light was filling the room he knew that for him, at least, talking would break the spell.

Last night he had told her everything, the words tumbling out of him like a high tide spilling over a breakwater. And now the water had drained away he felt as though he had been washed clean. He had never felt so calm, so utterly at ease with himself. Not even after the adoption had been finalised.

Everything felt right in the world.

His arm tightened around her as he remembered what he'd said to her after winning the Palio. *'When I'm with you, everything is right.'* He had been still in shock, dazed with victory, but it was true, nonetheless.

He couldn't imagine how life could get any better.

He couldn't imagine life without her.

But he was going to have to: she was leaving today.

He'd always known the day was coming, and in the beginning the end hadn't mattered. All he'd cared about was trapping her, making her come out here because he had known she didn't want to. These last few days he had simply ignored the passing of time. Now, though, perhaps out of spite, time had caught up with him in a rush.

That was why he had kept reaching for her in the growing light, knowing that she would soon be gone. Sleep would have been impossible. Now, though, he was awake, and time was running out.

So ask her to stay.

For a moment he lay listening to her heartbeat. He could ask her. All it would take was three little words: *Stay with me.*

But stay for what? Sex?

Talitha deserved more than that. But what else could he offer her? They might have shared their pasts, but that didn't mean they had a future together. He had made that mistake before, and hurt both of them in the process, and he wasn't about to hurt her again. So why squander their remaining time together in calculating imaginary scenarios?

'Maybe you need a prize.'

Talitha's voice broke across his thoughts and he looked down at her, his hand moving automatically to touch her. As his fingers traced the curve of her hip he felt her shiver, and he felt his own body tense.

'A prize for what?'

'For winning the Palio. Then you might dream about winning instead.'

He stared down at her, his heart jostling against his ribs. 'But I don't need to dream about winning. Because you're here…with me. You're my prize,' he said softly.

He pulled her against him, his lips finding hers, his hand drifting over her body, feeling her shiver again as his fingers brushed against the hard buds of her nipples.

Talitha moaned softly. She could feel herself melting and, unwilling to lose control so soon, she batted his hand away and dropped her mouth to his chest, sliding down the bed, kissing lower, then lower still, her fingers following her lips to where he was already rock-hard.

The desire to taste him, to hold him in her mouth and feel him grow, was almost overwhelming.

Heart hammering, she began to move her mouth over the smooth, blunt head of his erection. His head fell back, his fingers gripping her hair, and she felt him grow even harder as the blood surged into the wet, straining length of him.

With a groan, he raised her head from his lap, pulling her up the bed, lifting her, and heat spilled over her skin as she guided him into her body.

Talitha shuddered as he pressed his thumb against the taut, pouting nub of her clitoris, then lifted his head to suck fiercely on her nipples until she grew frantic in her movements.

'Yes, like that…' she panted.

She tensed, her back arching, and after rolling her under him Dante thrust into her. The aftershocks of her orgasm tightened around him as his body jerked forward in a series of mindless shuddering spasms.

'What are you looking at?'

Glancing up from her laptop, Talitha felt her heart swoop like a swallow as she looked at the man sitting beside her. Dante was so beautiful, so familiar to her, and as necessary now as the air she breathed. Only also like a swallow she would be returning home soon. Home for her was and had always been Ashburnham— but how would that work if her heart was here with Dante in Siena?

Then tell him how you feel, she told herself, for what had to be the hundredth time since she had woken this morning.

But that was easier said than done.

Last night, in the aftermath of his daunting confession, it hadn't been the right time. And even now she was still searching for the right words to tell him she loved him.

Liar, she accused herself silently.

The words were easy. What was making them stall in her throat was fear. What if Dante didn't feel the same? Her heart skipped a beat as she remembered the blaze in his eyes when his horse had crossed the finishing line.

'When I'm with you, everything is right.'

Everything felt more than right between them.

It felt perfect.

'It's a painting that's just come up for auction in London.' She turned the screen towards him. 'I know we talked about introducing some art to your offices. I thought this might be a good starting point.'

They had talked briefly about the possibility of making art central to the identity of KCX, of using it to connect with the public. But truthfully, it had been little more than a passing remark. What she'd really been doing was giving herself another reason not to go upstairs and pack her bags.

Heart pounding, she watched as he tilted the screen.

'It's a good idea,' he said slowly, handing back the laptop.

'Good.' She swallowed. 'I can set up a telephone bid for you.'

'Or...' reaching across the sofa, he caught her hand and tugged her towards him, his eyes steady on hers '...I could fly back to London with you and we could go to the auction together. And while I'm in England there's nothing to stop us carrying on as we are.'

The world went still.

Talitha stared at Dante, her heart beating slow and hard.

It wasn't a declaration or love—he wasn't even marking a change in their relationship status—but it didn't matter. It was enough that he was offering to come back to England with her, and she was suddenly so filled with happiness and relief that for a moment she couldn't speak.

'Will you stay at the Hanover?' she asked.

'Would that be easier?'

She nodded. 'My grandfather is pretty old-fashioned. And he gets confused.'

'It's okay, *ciccia*. I understand,' he said softly.

Looking into his eyes, she saw that he did, and she was suddenly almost overwhelmed with loving him. She laid her head on his shoulder so that he couldn't see her face.

'Would it be okay if I stayed over?' she asked.

She felt his lips brush against her hair.

'I thought you'd never ask.'

Looking up at him, she pulled his head down and kissed him hungrily, losing herself in the familiar contours of his mouth.

'But I want you to meet my grandfather. Actually, I want him to meet you.' She wanted Edward to meet the man who had saved his home, saved his granddaughter.

'Of course.'

There was a different note in his voice now, one that made her quiver inside, and then he lifted her hand and pressed it to his lips as if sealing the deal.

When Talitha went upstairs to pack, Dante went into his office and pulled open his laptop. Ostensibly he checked his emails every morning, but quite honestly the last few days he had just been going through the motions.

He leaned back in his seat. It wasn't as if he needed to work so hard. He had more money than he could spend, and the compulsion that had driven him for so long, the need to distance himself from the past, no longer seemed to matter now that Talitha knew the truth.

Obviously he wouldn't stop working, but he didn't need to work so hard. Now that Talitha was in his life he didn't want to work so hard…

His eyes froze on the screen, a name leaping out from the words around it as he breathed out unsteadily. Roger Dawson was the ex-marine who managed his security and kept an eye on the Cannavaro clan.

Opening the email, he read the three short sentences once, then reread them. The facts remained the same. His birth father and two of his brothers had been arrested for armed robbery.

There was a lead weight in his chest, pressing down on his lungs so that it was suddenly hard to breathe. He felt the familiar swirling rush of unfiltered emotion. Soon it would be followed by an exhaustion that made ordinary tasks impossible, but before that happened he would call his parents.

They alone understood how this made him feel.

Except this time he didn't even reach for the phone. Instead he got unsteadily to his feet. It was Talitha he wanted… Talitha he needed. And not just for sex, and not just in this moment.

He needed her because he loved her.

How could he not have realised?

He stumbled against the desk, his fingers tightening against the smooth wood not with shock but with acceptance. He loved her. Even when he'd hated her, even when he'd been too scared to let himself love or be loved, he'd loved her.

Heart thumping, he sat down again. And now he had a second chance. A chance to do it right—to love her as she deserved to be loved. His hands trembled against the desk. He felt suddenly close to tears. For so long he had kept to the shadows, but now there was a promise of light, a small but steady spark of hope.

Glancing back at the screen of his computer, he felt his tumbling thoughts stall. There was a second email. This time Roger was even more succinct.

Just to warn you, Il Giorno and Telecampania are running pieces on the Cannavaro family.

He stared at the screen, his blood banging clumsily through his veins like the horses in the *piazza* yesterday. It didn't have to matter. Talitha knew all about his past, and she had neither flinched nor turned away. On the contrary, she had embraced him, taken him into her body. And yet—

His shoulders tensed and he turned his gaze away from the screen, away from the truth he wanted to ignore, the truth he'd done everything in his power to shun, even going so far as to pretend that he and Talitha were different people.

But this wasn't a game of two strangers in a bar.

He slammed the laptop shut.

This was real life, Talitha's life, and she deserved better than this. Better than him.

And now he understood why it had taken him so long to realise that he loved her. It was because deep down he had always known this moment would happen. And that even if he managed to get past it, it would be just a matter of time before it happened again, and at some point this peace, this certainty would all be snatched away from him.

It was no good telling himself that it would change.

This was never going to stop.

There was always going to be another email, another robbery, another trial, and one day soon some reporter would join the dots, and then his past would be out there for the whole world to see and judge.

And if—*when*—it all went public, how would Talitha feel about him then? Here, now, who he was and where he came from felt very distant and contained. But would she really be able to turn away from the headlines? And how would she feel when she saw what it meant to be a Cannavaro? When she found out about their crimes? Could she really love a man who carried that chaos inside him?

More importantly, could he—*should* he—expect her to? She had so much to deal with already. He couldn't allow her to take him on as well. Not if he loved her—

and he did. And, loving her as he did, he couldn't put her in harm's way.

'Angelica says the car is ready.'

Talitha was standing in the doorway, her brown eyes hazy in the sunlight from the window. She smiled shyly and he had to look away, for fear of betraying the ache in his chest at the thought of her leaving and of what he was about to do. What he had to do.

'Slight change of plan,' he said quickly. 'Something's come up. I've got a couple of conference calls I need to join in on.'

He watched her reaction. Slight surprise followed by acceptance.

'Okay, shall I tell the driver to wait?'

Gritting his teeth, he shook his head. 'No, that won't be necessary. Don't let me hold you up.'

She stared at him, her smile fading now. 'I don't understand. What are you saying?'

'I can't come to London with you. I thought I could, but I can't.'

'Because of work?' she said slowly.

He nodded. 'I've already taken a lot of time off. Too much.'

The shock in her eyes almost made him change course, but he forced his gaze to stay steady.

'I thought you wanted this…us—' She broke off, frowning, then tried again. 'I thought we were going to carry on in London. You said there was no reason to stop.'

'I know what I said, but on second thoughts I think

it's more important to have a reason to carry on,' he said brusquely.

There was a long silence. Then, 'Yes, I suppose it is.'

The hurt in her eyes took his breath away, but he blanked his mind to her pain. 'In which case, now might be a good time for you to hand me over to your colleague. I know you had someone in mind.'

'Arielle.' Her voice was small and stunned.

'Good. I'll call Philip, let him know.'

For a moment she just stood there, staring at him, and then she said quietly, 'And that's what you want, is it? You want us to go our separate ways?'

He stared at her in silence, pain splintering through him as if she was twisting his heart in their hands. No, he didn't want that. But what he wanted was irrelevant. He had to do what was right.

'Talitha—'

'Because that's not what I want,' she said hoarsely. 'And I don't think you do either. I think you're scared. And I am too. But I'm more scared of not being with you.' Her fingers caught his. 'Because I love you and I want us to be together.'

Could she ratchet up the pain any tighter? His jaw clenched. It was agony, hearing her offer her love, but she was right. He was scared. Scared of loving her and losing her again or, worse, of pulling her down into the darkness with him.

He pulled his fingers free. 'I'm sorry, Talitha, but I don't love you,' he lied. 'I'm sorry if anything I did led you to think differently, but it's probably best we call it a day now rather than carry on.'

Their eyes met then. For a moment she didn't speak, and then she nodded slowly.

'Yes, it is. You see, I want more. I want more than just carrying on with or without a reason. And I don't think you're capable or willing to give more. Goodbye, Dante,' she said quietly, and then she turned and walked out of his office.

CHAPTER TEN

LEANING INTO THE ROAD, Talitha held up her hand. 'Oh, you have to be kidding—'

She swore as the black cab trundling down Regent Street abruptly signalled left and disappeared down a side street. That was the third taxi in as many minutes, but it was also the final straw, and if there had been a camel standing on the pavement beside it would have sat down by now, moaning in despair.

It had been a terrible day at the end of an appalling week. The plumbing at Ashburnham had finally dried up completely this morning, she had narrowly missed out on a painting, losing to Dubarry's main rivals, Broussard's, and to top it all she had just caught the heel of one of her favourite shoes in a crack in the pavement.

Glancing up at the darkening sky, she gritted her teeth. Now it was going to rain, and she had left her umbrella at work. She watched miserably as a fourth taxi appeared in the distance. It was no good, it didn't have its light on…

Oh, thank you, thank you, she crooned silently as it

drew up in front of Gusto, the authentically Hispanic tapas restaurant currently wowing London's diners, and deposited a well-dressed couple on the pavement.

She felt the first fat drops of rain explode against her face, and by the time she reached the shuddering black car, limping as far as her broken heel would allow, she was soaked through.

'Where to, love?' the driver shouted above the rain, which was sheeting down now, streaming off the windscreen as if they were in the middle of a car wash.

She gave him the address and slumped back against the seat, the sound of the rain fading into the background as she stared down at her dress. The pale fabric was clinging to her body and she had a sudden vivid flashback to the moment in the rowing boat when she had kissed Dante.

Her fingers tightened in her lap.

That had been the tipping point, the moment of choice. Except 'choice' implied options, and there had never been any real choice to make. Not on her part anyway.

Not until the end.

Lifting her face, she gazed blankly through the window at the saturated streets, watching the pedestrians scamper from doorway to doorway. They were shielding themselves from the worst of the downpour with umbrellas and folded newspapers and briefcases, and that was what she had done.

She had shielded herself from further hurt.

Would it have made any difference if she had refused to leave?

She was sure not, and yet even now, a week after she had walked out of Dante's villa, and out of his life, a part of her wished she had been brave enough to stay and fight.

But was it brave or just stupid to offer up the most beautiful, fragile, precious piece of yourself to someone who didn't and would never love you? And if she was sure of one thing it was that Dante didn't, and couldn't love her.

The journey home had been appalling. Sitting hunched in her seat, alone on Dante's jet, she had never felt more worthless or unhappy. With every passing cloud the ache in her chest had deepened and only the last remnants of her pride had stopped her from buckling beneath the sympathetic but unspoken pity of the stewards.

Back in London, she had gone straight to the townhouse, and it had been there that she had finally given in to what she had wanted to do since Dante had made his 'slight change' to their plans, and cried. Great, wrenching sobs—not just because she had loved and lost Dante again, but because there was no more hope.

That was the difference from last time. After Milan, outwardly at least, she had learned to live without him, without his passion, but she hadn't ever really let go of her dream of love.

Her heart twisted as the taxi turned into Ashburnham's long tree-lined drive. She could still taste him in her mouth, feel the urgent push of his body inside hers. And she still loved him. Maybe she always would.

But she had accepted that her love alone wasn't

enough to make their relationship work. That blaze in his eyes after the Palio had been triumph, not love, and that was why, this time, it really was goodbye not *ciao*.

The taxi came to a standstill and, leaning forward, she paid the driver.

Outside the rain had stopped, and she let herself in to the house. Glancing into the drawing room, she saw that her grandfather was asleep in his chair by the window and so, tiptoeing back out of the room, she made her way upstairs, some of her misery lifting as she remembered his reaction when she'd got home.

It was true that he'd thought she had just come in from work, but he'd been delighted to see her, and his happiness had gone some way to restoring her equilibrium, as had the knowledge that their home was safe.

She had been dreading work, or more specifically the curiosity of her colleagues about Dubarry's most secretive client, but with a huge auction of German expressionist art only days away everyone had been too busy to do more than smile and congratulate her.

Except Philip, who had been so pleased with her that he was promising a pay rise.

Her shoulders tightened. Perhaps that was why he was holding back on telling her that Arielle would be working with Dante from now on.

Folding her arm across the ache in her chest, she stared at the picture of Cinderella on her wall. It was her favourite scene in the book—the one where the fairy godmother conjured a coach from a pumpkin and turned ragged clothes into a ball gown fit for a princess to dance with a prince.

Maybe that was where she'd gone wrong, she thought sadly, tracing the outline of the dress with her finger. She should have settled for a prince instead of falling in love with a King.

Lifting the oars out of the water, Dante stepped out of the boat and onto the island. Heart pounding, he stared up at the sky, looking at but not really seeing the crescent moon. He had no idea what time it was. No idea how long he had been prowling the estate in the darkness. Nor did he really care.

Except that he should care.

The last few days he had let things slip, but tomorrow he was flying back to the States. He had a week of back-to-back meetings lined up and he needed to be on his game. What he didn't need was to be wandering about here in the dark. He should be in bed asleep.

Sleep! He almost laughed out loud.

He hadn't slept since Talitha left. He went to bed each night, but all that happened was that he lay there in the darkness as if she were there beside him, her soft, pale body shifting against the sheets, her hand moving with tantalising lightness over the contours of his chest, one finger tracing the line of hair down to his groin—

His jaw clenched. Tonight, he'd had enough. If Talitha wouldn't leave him alone, he would leave her in the bedroom.

But of course she had followed him, just as she did in the daytime. He could be eating his breakfast and catch a glimpse of her in the silver handle of his spoon, or see her face reflected over his shoulder as he pretended to work on his laptop. Just moments ago he had stumbled to a halt as he came across her, standing on one leg, a sketchbook in her hand, her teeth biting into her lower lip.

He had tried everything to evade her. Reading, writing, working out in his gym until he was drenched in sweat and had to lean against the treadmill like some punch-drunk boxer at the end of his career.

When none of that had worked he'd tried just closing his eyes, but that only made everything worse. Then there was no escape. Inside his head she was impossible to resist, and he tormented himself, replaying every movement and gesture she'd made in slow motion.

And if that wasn't agonising enough, to rub salt into the wound all through the week works of art had been arriving, in innocuous-looking royal blue crates with *lato da aprire* stencilled on them in yellow lettering. *Open this side.*

The truth was that it didn't matter how he looked at his life—there was no way out. He was locked in an inferno of his own making.

His eyes fixed on the bare marble plinth in the middle of the temple. His new Diana was yet to arrive, but she wasn't the woman he was missing.

The woman he wanted.

The woman he needed.

After he'd read that email from Roger he had wanted to take Talitha into his arms, but he hadn't. Even after she'd told him that she wanted more. For both their sakes he had pushed her away, telling himself that it was for the best.

Only how could it be for the best when it was Talitha who made him whole?

An ache was building in his chest. He remembered how she had stood before him and offered him her love. Unconditionally and completely. When she'd left she had taken the most vital and precious part of him with her. But it had taken her leaving for him to understand that, and now it was too late.

The oars trembled in his hands.

Then again, London was an hour behind Siena…

Thank goodness it was the weekend tomorrow, Talitha though, dumping her bag on the settle by the door and slipping off her shoes. The summer storms from earlier in the week had given way to a heatwave, and today was officially the hottest day of the year.

Because Philip was such a good boss, he had let everyone leave early, and all the way home she had been promising herself a dip in the lake. But first she would check on her grandfather. Make sure he was wearing his hat.

Her chest squeezed tight. If he was in good form then she might broach the subject that she had been putting off since yesterday.

It was time to make a change. She'd accepted that even before Dante had stormed back into her life, and while their situation might be less perilous than before, they still couldn't afford to keep two houses running. Her plan to sell the townhouse would give them the financial security they both needed and she craved, and so yesterday morning she had spoken to an estate agent and a lawyer.

That left Ashburnham.

She bit her lip. This part was going to be trickier to run past her grandfather, although she knew it made perfect sense. Between the two of them, they only really used about a quarter of the house, so why not hand over the rest to the British Heritage Trust? That way Ashburnham would not just be looked after, it would be filled with visitors again. and her grandfather would still be able to keep living in his home.

If she could just find the right words…

Her footsteps faltered and she frowned as male voices floated towards her through the house.

That was odd. Jill was working today, not Michael. Unless they had changed shifts. Or the plumber had finally decided to turn up. He had managed to sort out almost everything else, but he'd had to order a part for the shower.

She felt a flurry of panic. Would her grandfather remember that? Or even remember the plumber?

She hurried through the French windows onto the terrace—and stopped abruptly, every muscle, every nerve, every fibre of her being stretched to breaking point.

Her grandfather was sitting in his usual chair, an open copy of the *Racing Post* in his lap. On the table next to him a bottle of champagne sat in a bucket of ice, and on the other side of the table was a man wearing jeans and a T-shirt that showcased the hard muscles of his arms and chest.

Her heartbeat accelerated as she stood frozen in the warm afternoon sunlight. He might be dressed casually, and he quite possibly knew how to fix a shower, but he wasn't the plumber.

She had thought about Dante endlessly this past week, playing out an inconceivable number of conversations with him inside her head, but now that he was sitting on her terrace she could only stand and stare. She couldn't understand how he could be here. It didn't make any sense.

This was her world. Her home. Her grandfather.

The same grandfather who was currently sharing a glass of champagne with a stranger.

She let go of the breath she'd been holding.

Happily sharing.

Edward looked flushed with excitement, and younger than he had in years.

Forcing herself to put one leg in front of the other, she walked over to her grandfather.

'Talitha, darling—there you are.'

His voice tugged her gaze towards him and, leaning forward, she kissed his cheek.

'I know it's a little early, but Dante just told me about his win at the Palio and I thought we should celebrate.'

She blinked. *Dante?*

Not Mr King, but Dante.

With an effort, she lifted her face to meet his. Her breath caught in her throat. As usual, the curves of his face looked miraculous, but there were dark smudges under his eyes and he seemed thinner.

'Talitha, darling. Why don't you get another glass and join us?'

Turning swiftly to her grandfather, she shook her head, smiling stiffly. 'It's fine, Grandpa. I don't want one.'

'I can get you a glass.'

Her head whipped round and she glowered at Dante. 'I can get my own glass, thank you.'

'Good girl.' Her grandfather patted her on the arm. 'Why don't you take Dante with you? You can show him the painting of the Pearl.'

Head spinning, she took a breath, trying to stay calm. Her grandfather was sweetly excited, but she just wanted this strange walking-on-eggshells encounter to be over.

'Grandpa, Mr King is a very busy man.' She flicked a glance in Dante's direction. 'I'm sure he has other plans.'

There was a small pause, and then Dante shook his head. 'Not at all. Your grandfather has been telling me all about his horses. I'd be delighted to see the painting.'

Her lips tightened. For a moment she considered up-ending the ice bucket on his head, but then her spine sagged. She couldn't fight both of them.

'Fine. If you'd like to follow me?' She stalked past Dante with her nose in the air.

'Talitha—' He caught up with her by the staircase. 'I'm sorry to turn up unannounced,' he said quietly.

'Not as sorry as I am,' she snapped. 'What are you doing here?'

'I need to talk to you.'

Now he wanted to talk?

She felt her stomach flip over.

'It's not really office hours, Mr King.' Hating how her voice was high and twisted, she turned and stomped up the stairs to the first-floor landing. 'Here. This is the Pearl.' She gestured towards the painting of the grey racehorse. 'Now you've seen him, you can go back downstairs and tell my grandfather that you're very sorry but you have to leave right away.'

He stared at her steadily. 'You don't think that'll look a little odd? I mean, what could possibly be that urgent?'

He sounded so calm and controlled that she felt almost sick. She pretended to think. 'Well, they say that if you want someone to believe you when you're lying you should stick as close to the truth as possible, so I guess it would probably be something to do with work. I mean, that's always your number one priority, isn't it, Dante?'

His eyes were fixed on her face. 'I haven't done a stroke of work for weeks. Not since I walked into Dubarry's and saw you standing in front of that painting.'

'And that's my fault, is it?'

'That's not what I'm saying.'

'But you're thinking it,' she said flatly. 'So what is it you want to say?'

Looking up at him, she felt her throat contract. She already knew the answer. His face was taut and there was a rigidity in how he was holding himself. He wanted the last word.

'I'm saying that I don't care about work.' His mouth twisted. 'I don't care about art. I don't care about the Palio. None of it matters. It's you that I care about, Talitha. You that I love.'

She stared at him blankly. Inside her she could feel a thousand tiny flowers of hope blossoming, their petals opening, delicate as butterfly wings. But she must have misheard him.

Say it again, she thought. But she couldn't ask. She wanted to spin out the fantasy just a little longer.

Gazing down into Talitha's pale, wary face, Dante took a breath. He felt as though his whole life had been building to this moment of truth and trust, and he was suddenly terrified that he would mess it up.

'I don't think I ever stopped loving you. That's why I haven't been with another woman since you left Milan. I couldn't. No one ever came close to you.'

Talitha didn't say anything, but he could tell that she was stunned by his confession.

'You haven't been with anyone…?' Her voice was like air.

Taking a step closer, he shook his head. He didn't care about his ego. Too many times he had let doubt into their relationship and it wasn't going to happen again.

'Why do you think I was so out of control in the boat? Right from the first time we met there was only ever you.'

'You're just talking about sex,' she said flatly.

'I'm not.' He took another step closer. 'I love you, Talitha. I didn't want to. I didn't think I could. But I can't not. Even when you're not with me I'm with you. I eat with you. Walk with you. Sleep with you. I even brush my teeth with you. Every thought I have begins and ends with you. You fill my head. You fill my heart.'

Her face trembled. 'So why did you push me away?'

He ran a hand over his face. 'My whole life I've been scared of my family catching up with me. It's why I've worked so hard. It's even why I wanted an art collection. It felt like I was building a wall. Only then I realised I loved you, and that if I followed my heart then my past would become *your* past, and I couldn't bear the idea of you having to deal with it too.'

Heart hammering in his chest, he stared down into her eyes.

'But then, when I talked to you, I felt better…stronger.' His eyes found hers. 'You made me see that I didn't have to run any more. Or lie or hide.'

Reaching into the pocket of his jeans, he pulled out his phone.

'I should have done this three years ago. I wish I had. But I spoke to my PR department this morning and we worked on this together. It went out on the KCX website at lunchtime.'

Talitha stared at the screen. At the top of the page was a piece about a new arts hub in Naples, the first in a series of specially commissioned spaces to be built in deprived areas that would be funded by KCX. It was followed by a statement from KCX's CEO, Dante King, revealing his very personal reasons for funding the project.

Talitha looked up at him mutely, deprived of the powers of speech again. Not by anger this time, but by love. 'Oh, Dante...'

Letting out a long quiver of breath, she stepped closer, taking his hands in hers.

'*Wait.*'

She heard him swallow, and he pulled his hands free and reached into his pocket again.

'In Siena you said you wanted more—more than I was capable or willing to give. And I know it's probably too late, but that's why I'm here. I had to tell you that I *am* capable and willing, only I know that's not enough. I know you need more. I can't just tell you. I need to show you how I feel.'

Looking down, she felt her breath catch. The ring lying in his hand was both familiar and different.

'I had it reset. I didn't want to forget how we got here.' He pointed out the three sparkling sapphires. 'But I wanted to add something to mark the journey we've taken.'

His eyes were blazing like they had after the Palio, but this time she knew that she was the reason.

'I love you Talitha.'

'And I love you too.' Tears were streaming down her face. 'When I'm not with you it feels like I'm drowning,' she said shakily.

Leaning forward, he kissed her as he had at the

Palio, kissed her until she was floating, not drowning, until finally they broke apart to catch their breath.

'You hold my heart in your hands,' he said softly. 'Please let me hold yours. Please will you be my wife?'

There was a long, pulsing silence. She knew Dante was staring at her, waiting for her to react, but her brain seemed to have shut down. Or perhaps it was too busy fighting the sudden wild beating of her heart.

'Yes…' she whispered, and as he slid the ring on her finger the love and certainty in his eyes filled her with a happiness that was as pure and warm and unwavering as the sunlight streaming through the window.

* * * * *

Caught up in the magic of
The Italian's Runaway Cinderella?
Why not get lost in these other Louise Fuller stories?

The Rules of His Baby Bargain
The Man She Should Have Married
Italian's Scandalous Marriage Plan
Beauty in the Billionaire's Bed
The Christmas She Married the Playboy

Available now!

#3993 PENNILESS AND PREGNANT IN PARADISE
Jet-Set Billionaires
by Sharon Kendrick

One extraordinary Balinese night in the arms of guarded billionaire Santiago shakes up Kitty's life forever! She'll confess she's pregnant, but she'll need more than their scorching chemistry to accept his convenient proposal!

#3994 THE ROYAL BABY HE MUST CLAIM
Jet-Set Billionaires
by Jadesola James

When a scandalous night results in a shock baby, Princess Kemi ends up wearing tycoon Luke's ring! She fears she's swapping gilded cages as she struggles to break into his impenetrable heart. But will their Seychelles honeymoon set her free?

#3995 INNOCENT IN THE SICILIAN'S PALAZZO
Jet-Set Billionaires
by Kim Lawrence

Soren Steinsson-Vitale knows Anna Randall is totally off-limits. She's his sworn enemy's granddaughter and he's also her boss. But one kiss promises a wild connection that will lead them straight to his palazzo bedroom!

#3996 REVEALING HER NINE-MONTH SECRET
Jet-Set Billionaires
by Natalie Anderson

After one magical evening ended in disaster, Carrie assumed she'd never see superrich Massimo again. So, a glimpse of him nine months later sends her into labor—with the secret she didn't know she was carrying!

HPCNMRA0222

#3997 CINDERELLA FOR THE MIAMI PLAYBOY
Jet-Set Billionaires
by Dani Collins

Bianca Palmer's world hasn't been the same since going into hiding and becoming a housekeeper. So, she's shocked to discover her boss is Everett Drake—the man she shared a mesmerizing encounter with six months ago! And their attraction is just as untamable...

#3998 THEIR ONE-NIGHT RIO REUNION
Jet-Set Billionaires
by Abby Green

When Ana conveniently wed tycoon Caio, they were clear on the terms: one year to expand his empire and secure her freedom. But as the ink dries on their divorce papers, they're forced together for twenty-four hours...and an unrealized passion threatens to combust!

#3999 SNOWBOUND WITH HIS FORBIDDEN PRINCESS
Jet-Set Billionaires
by Pippa Roscoe

Princess Freya is dreading facing Kjell Bergqvist again. He's nothing like the man who broke her heart eight years ago. But memories of what they once shared enflame new desires when a snowstorm leaves them scandalously, irresistibly stranded...

#4000 RETURN OF THE OUTBACK BILLIONAIRE
Jet-Set Billionaires
by Kelly Hunter

Seven years ago, Judah Blake took the fall for a crime he didn't commit to save Bridie Starr. Now his family's land is in *her* hands, and to reclaim his slice of the Australian outback, he'll claim her!

YOU CAN FIND MORE INFORMATION ON UPCOMING HARLEQUIN TITLES, FREE EXCERPTS AND MORE AT HARLEQUIN.COM.

She needed him to turn. Would she see those disturbingly green
eyes? Would she see a sensual mouth? If he stepped closer would
she hear a voice that whispered wicked invitation and willful
temptation? All those months ago she'd been so seduced by him
she'd abandoned all caution, all reticence for a single night of
silken ecstasy only to then—

A sharp pain lanced, shocking her back to the present. Winded,
she pressed her hand to her stomach. How the mind could wreak
havoc on the body. The stabbing sensation was a visceral reminder
of the desolate emptiness she'd been trying to ignore for so long.

She'd recovered from that heartbreak. She was living her best
life here—free and adventurous, bathing in the warm, brilliant
waters of the Pacific. Her confusion was because she was tired.
But she couldn't resist stepping closer—even as another sharp pain
stole her breath.

"That's interesting." He addressed the man beside him. "Why
are—"

Shock deadened her senses, muting both him and the pain still
squeezing her to the point where she couldn't breathe. That *voice*?
That low tone that invited such confidence and tempted the listener
to share their deepest secrets?

Massimo hadn't just spoken to her. He'd offered the sort of attention that simply stupefied her mind and left her able only to say *yes*. And she had. Like all the women who'd come before her. And doubtless all those after.

Now his brief laugh was deep and infectious. Despite her distance, it was as if he had his head intimately close to hers, his arm around her waist, his lips brushing her highly sensitized skin—

Pain tore through her muscles, forcing her to the present again. She gasped as it seared from her insides and radiated out with increasingly harsh intensity. She stared, helpless to the power of it as that dark head turned in her direction. His green-eyed gaze arrowed on her.

Massimo.

"Carrie?" Sereana materialized, blocking him from her view. "Are you okay?" Her boss looked as alarmed as she sounded.

Carrie crumpled as the cramp intensified. It was as if she'd been grabbed by a ginormous shark and he was trying to tear her in two. "Maybe I ate something…"

Her vision tunneled as she tumbled to the ground.

"Carrie?"

Not Sereana.

She opened her eyes and stared straight into his. "Massimo?"

It couldn't really be him. She was hallucinating, surely. But she felt strong arms close about her. She felt herself lifted and pressed to his broad, hard chest. He was hot and she could hear the thud of his racing heart. Or maybe it was only her own.

If this were just a dream? Fine. She closed her eyes and kept them closed. She would sleep and this awful agony would stop. She really needed it to stop.

"Carrie!"

Don't miss
Revealing Her Nine-Month Secret,
available April 2022 wherever
Harlequin Presents books and ebooks are sold.

Harlequin.com